TREASURES
OF THE HEART

TREASURES
OF THE HEART

•

Terry Zahniser
McDermid

AVALON BOOKS
NEW YORK

PRINTED IN THE UNITED STATES OF AMERICA
ON ACID-FREE PAPER
BY HADDON CRAFTSMEN, BLOOMSBURG, PENNSYLVANIA

To Mom, Nadine, and Liz, for always believing I could do this.
And to Bob, David, and John, for encouraging me.

Chapter One

Tessa Montgomery clutched the handle of her briefcase as she walked down the hallway of the recently renovated city hall building, her stomach fluttering with excitement. Finding that newspaper article had been a stroke of luck. Now she should have no trouble convincing the committee that this was the perfect year to have the first annual Durant Founders Day Festival.

And they would finally think of her as an adult.

You are an adult, she reminded herself. *You've owned your own business for two years now and everything is going great. They wouldn't even have this committee if you hadn't organized things. So what if a few people still treat you like a child? They've watched you grow up and it's hard to see things differently sometimes.*

She was determined to help the town grow. Everything she needed was here in Durant and she couldn't imagine living anywhere else. If she moved, she probably wouldn't have to contend with people who remembered her as a toddler or a curious little girl. But her great-grandparents had helped found the community and she felt both pride and love for the town.

Outside the conference room, she straightened her shoulders under her jacket and stiffened her spine. She had spent several long minutes before the mirror trying to achieve the right degree of professionalism and approachability. Her long black hair was as neat as it could be in the twisted braid she had fashioned at the back of her head and her makeup was lightly applied, bringing out tiny flecks of green in her brown eyes.

After the bright lights of the hallway, she blinked several times to adjust to the dim light of the room. Only the middle bank of lights had been switched on. Blinking again, she turned toward the panel next to the door and lifted her hand toward the switch.

"Something in your eye, munchkin?" a deep voice drawled from her right side.

She jumped and just managed to swallow down her automatic retort. Smoothing her free hand down her skirt, she mentally counted to ten. She could handle this. He was not going to get a reaction out of her, not tonight of all nights.

She turned on the rest of the recessed lighting before turning around. Curving her lips upward in what she hoped passed for a smile, she met his familiar moss-green gaze.

"Hello, Luke. I didn't expect to see you here."

Her voice sounded normal and she breathed a silent prayer of relief. Of all people, Luke Hunter, here at the meeting! Not that the meetings weren't open to the public. But why did he have to come tonight? He'd never been to a meeting before.

He waved an arm toward the people milling around the

wide table that dominated the room. "This is where the Durant Business Committee meets?"

She nodded, not quite trusting her voice again, and waited for him to make the next comment, glancing sideways around the room, looking for an escape. No one seemed particularly aware of the two of them. All of the people already in the room were storeowners she recognized. Two women and a man stood near the floor-length tan drapes that covered the long windows of the wall opposite the door where she stood, their faces animated in conversation. Another woman and three men sat on one side of the table, cups of coffee in front of them and their notebooks already opened.

Luke didn't say anything and she wondered if it would be polite to just walk away. Just because she had known him for years didn't mean she had to stand there and converse with him. She needed time to gather her thoughts, think about her presentation.

The folder in her hand gave her courage. "If you'll excuse me," she said quietly, "the meeting should be starting pretty soon. I need to find a seat."

She turned but he caught her arm before she could walk away. "Could you answer a few questions first?" he asked, his voice low.

Surprised, she glanced at his hand on her sleeve, feeling the warmth of his fingers seeping under the light material and onto her skin. Not that he was holding her that tight. It was just odd, she told herself. Luke never touched her.

Before she could consider that fact more, he released her and stepped away. She carefully smoothed her hand down the lightly wrinkled material of her sleeve, brushing away his fingerprints, absorbing them into her skin. What a strange thought!

She tilted her chin up and met his steady gaze. "What do you want to know?"

"About this committee. Sam invited me, practically begged me to be here, but until he said something, I didn't even know there was a Durant Business Committee." He shrugged and gave her a rueful grin. "I don't think it would look good for the public school system if the high school social studies teacher isn't even aware of the local business organizations."

So he was here for information. She wasn't surprised Sam Green had invited him. Before the older man had opened Sports Shack, he had coached the most winning track teams in the history of the high school. Luke had been on the team during the last years of Sam's teaching career and they had stayed close over the years. Sam's retirement had opened up the position that Luke had taken at the high school.

As owner of the new Sports Shack, Coach Green was a vital part of the new committee. His store had opened down the street from her own and over the last few months, they had spent hours discussing the concerns of owning a small business. Listening to him had been one of the reasons she had first considered the committee.

"The DBC has only met three times so far, mostly to get organized," she said to Luke. "Our main emphasis is helping businesses succeed, especially in the downtown area. If people are shopping in one of our stores, that could draw them into the others."

He rubbed his chin with one hand. "You scratch my back, I'll scratch yours?"

She didn't know if she liked his description. "It goes deeper than that. We want to improve the downtown area, keep people here instead of them going to Tulsa or Joplin or even Kansas City. And with the growth in the Branson area, we're looking at ways to draw in some of the tourists traveling through town."

He nodded again. "Ambitious. How did it get started?"

She slanted him a sideways glance, wondering if he was baiting her. Did he know she had started the committee? His expression was bland but she had been fooled by him before.

"After talking with Coach Green about his concerns and finding that they were the same as the ones I had when I was starting out, I wondered if there would be any interest in a group forming that could help one another," she explained carefully. "The committee would allow new owners to ask questions and long-term shopkeepers could share their expertise. Most people I talked with were very interested, and so we had our first meeting."

"You organized the group?"

He didn't have to sound so surprised. "I did get a business administration degree at college, and Treasure Seekers' Haven is doing very well, thank you."

He lifted a hand in defense. "I'm not saying you couldn't do it. I'm just surprised Christine never said anything about it."

"Oh." She bit her lip, wondering what to say next. "She may not know about it," she finally managed, wondering if his sister did know about her new venture. Since Christine's marriage, they didn't spend as much time together. Had the topic ever come up in their conversations? "We're still pretty new and I'm not chairperson or anything."

"Oh, really?"

Tessa shook her head. "I didn't want the job." At least that would let him know she had been offered the position by the committee members who had attended the first meeting. "Helen White agreed to take the position. She probably has more experience than most of us put together and she knows more about this town than anybody."

"And what she doesn't know, she can easily find out," he whispered.

A startled snicker slipped over Tessa's lips and she pressed her fingers to her mouth, shaking her head at him. "Luke!" She glanced around quickly, hoping no one had overheard his comment.

"What? It's true. I bet she knows everything that goes on in this town."

"Maybe," she muttered, her voice muffled by her hand. As owner of the Cutting Edge Beauty Shop, it was true that gossip was as much a part of Helen's daily life as perms and hair rollers. But Luke didn't have to be so blunt, especially when Tessa was trying to project a professional image.

She turned away from him, trying to swallow the laughter that kept threatening to explode. He looked so innocent, like he didn't understand why she had found his comment so funny or why she would be upset with him. As if he didn't know!

Helen asked the group to take their seats and Tessa gave a silent thanks, walking toward the closest side of the table and pulling out one of the high-backed chairs in the middle of the row. She settled her folder on the table in front of her and sat down before she realized Luke had slid into the chair right next to her.

"What are you doing?" she whispered.

He gave her a puzzled look. "Sitting down."

"I know, but why there?"

He glanced around the table. A few folders sat on the

table on their side but most of the chairs were still empty. "Nobody else is sitting here."

She swallowed and forced her lips to smile. "The store owners sit at the table," she said carefully. "They're the only ones who can vote. Other interested parties sit in the chairs at the back of the room." She nodded toward the rows behind them. Not that she expected anyone to be sitting there. They had been empty during the last three meetings. During city council and school board meetings, they tended to have a few occupants, but the DBC was still a relatively new component of the city.

Before Luke could reply, an older man slid into the seat on the other side of Tessa. He leaned past her, his hand stretched toward Luke. "Hey, Luke, glad you could make it." He settled back in his chair and gave Tessa a broad smile. "Heard you have some interesting news."

Tessa gave him a warm smile. Sam Green had always been one of her favorite people. "I think so. But you'll have to wait like everyone else."

He laughed, a deep chuckle that she had heard for most of her teen years. In addition to coaching the track teams, he had been one of the most popular teachers at the high school, and his retirement had meant a lot of students would miss the intense discussions that made his social studies and government classes so interesting. He hadn't let anyone slack off in his class and she had benefited as much as the other students from his zeal, appreciating his rich sense of humor and his dedication to his students.

After the death of his wife three years earlier, he sold the small farm they owned outside town, moved into an apartment, and later bought an empty building on the same side of the street as Tessa's shop. The Sports Shack sold new and used sports equipment and athletic shoes and clothing. Making the transition from student to colleague had been challenging and Tessa still found it difficult not to call him Coach Green.

"Is Tom going to make it?" Sam asked Luke, referring to another former runner who now worked at the post office.

He shook his head. "The baby was sick and he didn't like leaving Kelly alone."

"Sorry to hear that." Sam leaned back and stretched his long legs out. "Tessa tell you about our last couple of meetings?"

Luke matched the coach's relaxed position. "Not yet."

"Hey, guys, I'm right here," she said, smiling at the coach. "We didn't have time for much except a little history of the group."

"Which is right up both your alleys," he said.

Tessa frowned at him. "History," the coach explained. "Your shop, his degree."

She looked at Luke in astonishment. She had never considered that they had a common interest in history. Luke was known around town for his coaching abilities and she hadn't thought much about what he taught in school. But he had taken Sam Green's position, so it made sense he would be teaching the social studies and history courses at the high school.

"She wouldn't give herself much credit anyway," Sam continued. "Instead of having the rest of us muddle around like she had to when she was starting out, she thought we should help one another. Next thing we knew, she had organized a group to help new owners by sharing the expertise of the more established owners."

Heat rose up her neck. Helen called the meeting to order before Tessa had time to reply and she quickly turned toward the front of the room. Criticism she could deal with easily. Compliments threw her into confusion every time.

No one asked Luke to move or made any comment about him sitting at the table with them, so Tessa kept her mouth shut. The chairs for visitors remained empty and there were enough seats around the table to comfortably fit in the entire group with several still empty after the first few minutes of the meeting.

Which was one of the problems, she thought, listening as announcements about upcoming sales and activities at their businesses were made by different members. The downtown was dying. Her block was one of the fortunate ones, with businesses in most of the buildings. Two blocks away, at the edge of downtown, the majority of the buildings stood unoccupied.

Luke's chair squeaked next to her and paper rustled as the minutes of the last meeting were handed out. She shifted her attention back to the room. As he handed her a copy of the minutes, the scent of his aftershave drifted toward her. He'd worn the same cologne for as long as she could remember, a deep, woodsy scent that conjured up long walks outside, fresh air. . . .

She shook her head and tried to concentrate on the minutes, listening to the low monotone and ignoring the steady sound of Luke's breathing just inches away from her.

With a pulse pounding near her right eye, she swallowed and stared at the words on the paper in front of her. What was the matter with her? Next to going to her shop every morning, she liked coming to the committee meetings, listening to the latest news, sharing with the other business owners. While she would never admit it out loud, they felt like family.

She was not going to let Luke Hunter distract her. He was her best friend's older brother and had been the torment of her childhood. She hadn't seen him much over the last few years, but whenever she did, she immediately felt like she was in elementary school again, wishing Christine's big brother would notice her and then melting with embarrassment when he did.

And his greeting hadn't helped. For as long as she could remember, he had called her "munchkin." At least he hadn't ruffled her hair this time like he used to.

Sam scooted his chair back from the table and interrupted her thoughts. She glanced at the agenda in front of her and saw that they were already considering committee reports.

Only two committees had been created, the group agreeing that it was better to start small and be successful than do too much too quickly. Sam headed a committee concerned with beautifying the downtown so that more people would be interested in shopping there.

"I've been getting some suggestions from the other owners," Sam said, handing around a stack of papers and indicating that each person should take one. "Flowerbeds, grassy areas, trees, benches for people to sit on and wait while someone is shopping."

Tessa picked up the neatly typed list. "Good thing he didn't write this himself," Luke whispered under the cover of the murmurs while people waited for their copies.

She choked on an involuntary giggle. For all his teaching skills, Coach Green's handwriting had been notoriously bad, his comments on papers almost indecipherable. He had usually appointed a student to write on the chalkboard and his handouts were typed by the school secretary.

She pressed her lips together and shifted away from

Luke. She was not in school anymore, gossiping in the back rows of the classroom. No one seemed to be paying any attention to their whispers but she was not going to take any chances.

"How much money are we talking about here?" Arthur Owens asked. The elderly man owned the variety store that had been a constant source of candy and small items since Tessa had been little.

"We're still gathering data," Sam said. "We have some ballpark figures but nothing firmed up yet. And until we know what people really want to do, we don't know which direction to go."

"Maybe we should hear from Tessa first before we make any other decisions," Helen suggested.

Sam nodded his head and moved back to his space at the table. "That'd be fine."

Tessa scooted her chair back and picked up her folder, aware of the many eyes on her. Her skin prickled and she swallowed before she found her earlier confidence. She couldn't stop a burst of satisfaction from spiraling through her, especially with Luke sitting next to her. "The committee liked the idea of having a Founders Day Festival for our downtown fund-raising event." She purposely kept her voice low-key as she handed around copies of the notes she had made. "And based on information I recently found, this will be a great year to start, since it will be the one hundredth birthday of Durant."

Excited murmurs flitted around the table. "One hundred is such a nice round number," she heard from across the way.

"A century of Durant," Martin Butterfield, the jeweler, chimed in.

"It wouldn't be right, though."

The murmuring died down. Tessa swung around and met Luke's gaze. "What?"

"The city isn't one hundred years old until next year," he said calmly.

"Oh, are you one of those who argued about when the millennium started?" Mabel Russell, owner of the clothing store for women and children, asked, an indulgent smile on her face.

Luke shook his head. "No, just going on the facts."

Tessa dug through the papers in her folder. "I'm using facts, too." She pulled out a single sheet of paper and waved it toward him. "This is a copy of the article that was in the paper when Durant celebrated its fiftieth birthday . . ." She waited a beat and then added, "fifty years ago."

She didn't do the obvious math for the group. Instead of the expected agreement with her, several were watching Luke with puzzled expressions on their faces. "Why don't you think this is the hundredth year?" Harold Gunderson, the local locksmith, finally asked.

Luke leaned forward, his elbows on the table. "I know most people probably think that the town was incorporated one hundred years ago." He gave Tessa an apologetic smile. "I thought the same thing until last year when I was doing some research for this year's school homecoming. We were going to emphasize the hundredth year because the first classes were held when the town was started," he explained to the interested group.

Tessa slid into her chair. The group had focused their attention on him and until he gave his information and the year of incorporation was settled, no one would want to listen to the other ideas she had gathered for the Founders Day celebration.

"James Durant regularly kept a diary during his lifetime, and I spent some time in the genealogical section of the library reading through them. He talked about the town and his hopes, why he came this way, what he planned to do," Luke continued.

Tessa glanced at him in surprise. She had never thought about him spending time with old books. She couldn't imagine many people having read the diaries of a man born over a hundred years ago. But how did this affect the date of the town's incorporation?

She didn't have long to wait. "In the back of one of the diaries was a letter," Luke continued. "It had been misplaced, put in a diary from James's later years. He had written the letter shortly after he arrived, and . . ." He hesitated and then stuck his hand into the pocket of his jeans. "Just a minute, let me read it to you."

"You carry the letter with you?" Tessa blurted as he drew out a single sheet of paper from his wallet.

From her position, she could see a dull red steal up his neck and disappear under the dark blond hair at his nape. "Not the actual letter. A copy." He carefully unfolded the letter and gave the group his customary grin. "I just think some of what he wrote was intriguing from an historical standpoint. And it's lucky I do carry a copy since it's important for this discussion."

He skimmed the paper for a few moments, the only sounds in the room the hum of the air conditioner and Arthur's cough. Luke smoothed the paper out and laid it on the table. "He wrote the letter to Phoebe, his fiancée back East. From what I understand in his diary, her parents had not been pleased with her choice of husband and so he had gone west to prove himself. Everything he did was to show

Phoebe and her family that he was a worthwhile candidate for her hand."

Tessa stared at him in fascination. His voice had changed and he was sitting very straight in his chair, his long fingers running down the words on the paper. Gone was the carefree man she usually saw. Passion for his subject flowed out of his mouth and she knew the rest of the group were as mesmerized as she was.

"He was excited about the prospects around here. He told Phoebe about some of the other people who were here. Your great-grandfather is mentioned," he said to Tessa. "And several other names I recognized from studying Durant history.

"The ending is the part that pertains to the Founders Day activities." He cleared his throat and picked up the letter, holding it in front of him. He read aloud:

"And so my dearest Phoebe, things are going very well here in Missouri. As soon as you arrive, we will become a town, ready for the future. I know that your parents, your father in particular, will want to know more of the details before they let you join me, so I have enclosed a separate page outlining the plans and have included several sketches done by a young man who recently arrived in town. I miss you, Phoebe, and am counting the days, not only for Durant, but for my own sake."

He stopped, the letter held between his fingers. A fascinated hush hung over the room. Mabel Russell broke the silence. "I don't understand."

"He promised her that he wouldn't incorporate the town without her," Luke said carefully, raising his head for the first time since he had started reading the letter. "He mentioned early in his first diary that he wanted her to be by his side when the occasion took place and referred to it several more times."

Tessa still couldn't get over the change in him. She knew that he was a favorite teacher. She had never considered that it could be because of his enthusiasm for his topic and the way he presented the information.

"But how does this prove that the town was incorporated a year later than people assume?" Wilson Pucket, the owner of Sole Repair, asked in a hushed voice.

"Their wedding date. Their tombstones include the years they were both born, died, and their wedding date. It's a year after the date we usually associate with the incorporation of Durant."

No one said anything. Tessa sat still, her mind spinning. Something bothered her about the letter but she didn't know what she wanted to ask.

"But how can we just accept a letter as proof?"

Tessa hadn't meant for her words to be so harsh and she quickly smiled at the surprised faces around her. "I don't dispute the letter," she said with a soft smile at Luke, "or that James wrote it, but how do we know he actually meant the town wouldn't be incorporated until he married Phoebe?"

"How do we know the facts in the newspaper article you cited are accurate?" he countered.

She forced herself to keep smiling. If the town wasn't 100 years old, most of her ideas for the festival wouldn't work. "The town has always used that date as the correct one."

Luke gave another of his shrugs. *He seems to do that a lot,* she thought irritably. *Like nothing I say is that impor-*

tant. "Common opinion doesn't make something right. The letter is a primary source. Your newspaper article is secondary. Does it even list where the information came from?"

Sam drummed his fingers on the table next to Tessa. "You know, in a way, you're both right," he put in.

Luke leaned forward. "How's that?"

"James *did* start the town a hundred years ago. According to your letter, Luke, it became official ninety-nine years ago."

Tessa tipped her head in acknowledgment, her arms folded over her chest. "That is one way of looking at things." She gave Luke a tight smile. Her plans for a hundred-year celebration could still work using Coach Green's logic.

"Then I make a motion that Luke Hunter and Tessa Montgomery act as co-chairpersons for the Founders Day Celebration this August."

Her smile vanished and she choked, leaning toward the older man. "Luke and I chair the committee together?" she managed through dry lips.

Sam nodded. "You don't have a problem with that, do you?"

How could she possibly tell this roomful of people that she always felt like she was still in grade school when she was around Luke? Admitting something like that would immediately lose her any respect she had gained over the past couple of years.

She gave a delicate shrug, only vaguely aware that she was using Luke's favorite form of response. Of course she could work with Luke. She could get along with anyone. She had always considered that to be one of her greatest strengths.

A nagging worry nudged its way into her brain. Not that she had ever been around Luke for prolonged periods of time. Usually he hadn't given his sister's friends more than a few moments of his precious time.

She swallowed and gave Sam a tight smile, glancing around the table at the expectant faces of the other members of the DBC. Catching a glimpse of the empty chairs in the back of the room, her mood lightened. But what if she didn't have to work with him?

"Of course I could work with Luke," she said, glad she could be so magnanimous now that she knew she wouldn't have to work with him. "But shouldn't the chairpersons both be from the Durant Business Committee? I mean, I know Luke is a public employee as a schoolteacher but since this committee is for business people . . ." She let her voice trail off and smiled gently at Sam before glancing at Luke, her eyebrows lifted slightly in challenge.

His mouth curved up at the corners, the twinkle in his eyes one she remembered all too well. "I guess Christine has been a little busy. She obviously hasn't told you that I'm part owner of the Sports Shack. I'm as much a committee member as you are, Tessa. And I think working on this committee with you will be fun."

Chapter Two

Tessa tossed ingredients into the bowl on the counter, her head tipped sideways as she tried to keep the phone on her shoulder. "Christine, why didn't you tell me Luke is part owner of the Sports Shack? First I find out the date I gave for the founding is wrong, and then I make a fool of myself because I thought Luke was just a visitor!"

"Tessa, calm down." Christine's patient voice came over the line. "You said yourself the date wasn't completely wrong. And I'm sure no one thought you were a fool. I don't know why you're so upset about this."

"Why I'm upset?" She chopped a tomato into minuscule pieces and added them to the shredded lettuce and diced carrots already in the bowl. "Christine, I have been working for the last two years to get those people to see me as an adult. And now I'm going to have to work with Luke and he'll undo everything I've done."

She knew she wasn't being entirely fair to Luke but she

didn't think she could easily work with him. No matter how much she had talked to herself during the night, she had found it difficult to remind herself that she wasn't the little friend of his sister anymore.

She took a deep breath and snapped the lid back on the salad dressing. She couldn't believe she hadn't emptied the entire contents onto the salad. Her heart was racing and she couldn't stop tapping her foot.

"I know he's your brother, Christine, but he makes me crazy.

"And that's another thing," Tessa snapped, holding the salad tongs just above the bowl. "Everybody always thinks I'm so calm and cool. And I am, usually. But just listen to me. Even talking about this makes me nuts."

"Maybe if you just ignored him, he wouldn't go out of his way to make you upset. It usually works for me."

"Usually," Tessa said, her attention fixed on the tree outside the kitchen window.

They weren't a committee of two, after all. At least four other people had volunteered to be on the new planning committee. With other people around, she would have a buffer.

"That still doesn't change the fact that this isn't the hundredth year," she muttered.

Christine laughed. "Tessa, before you found that article, you were just as excited about the Founders Day Festival. So it's not the hundredth year? That doesn't mean we can't have a great fund-raising activity. Oohh!" She gasped and then was silent.

"Christine?" Tessa stared at the receiver, all thoughts of her frustration with Luke disappearing. "Are you all right?"

"I'm fine." Christine's voice wafted faintly over the line.

"I just don't understand why they call this morning sickness."

Tessa breathed a tiny sigh of relief. "Did you talk to Mandy and Abby?"

"They were both disgustingly healthy during their entire pregnancies. In fact, Mandy had the nerve to say that she probably never felt better in her entire life."

Tessa swallowed a chuckle, covering the receiver with her hand, glad her friend couldn't see her face.

"And Jake isn't being any help at all," Christine continued.

"He isn't?" Tessa frowned at that. Jake doted on his wife. She couldn't imagine him not doing everything possible to help Christine feel better.

"He just asks if he can rub my feet and tells me to sit down, let him fix dinner. And Anna waits on me hand and foot."

This time, Tessa didn't hide her amusement and laughed out loud. "You big fake! You just don't want them making a big deal out of you being sickly."

"I'm not sickly!" Christine protested. "This is a normal biological process."

Tessa decided to take pity on her friend. "Tell you what, Christine. I'll come over tonight and watch Anna so you and Jake can go out and have a nice quiet dinner alone."

"Ohhh!" Another gasp. "Please, Tessa, don't mention food."

"Sorry. How about a movie? To get your mind off everything."

"It would be fun to go out. I mean, I love Anna and everything . . ." Her voice trailed off with a wistful little sigh.

"I know you do." No one who knew Christine could

doubt that she loved Jake's little sister. After the death of his mother and Anna's father, Jake had taken over the care of his young half-sister and Christine was determined to give her a childhood as full of love as her own had been.

"I'll be over in half an hour," Tessa said. "And don't worry about Anna's supper. I'll take care of it."

She hung up the phone and glanced at the bowl in front of her. The vegetables almost looked pureed. She gave them a quick toss with her fork and shuddered when they slithered back into the bowl with a soft plop.

"Definitely not edible." She dumped the soggy mess into the trash, rinsed the bowl, and went upstairs to her bedroom to change clothes.

Her folder for the committee sat on the dresser inside her room. She sighed. Her new ideas wouldn't work if they didn't use the one-hundred-year theme. Not that Luke would mind. He had smiled and murmured a few insincere comments about not wanting to jump into anything but she had seen right through him. He had shrugged once and suggested that maybe he wasn't the best choice for the co-chair position but he hadn't argued that long or that hard.

Her T-shirt half over her head, she paused. Why would he want to take on extra responsibility so close to the end of the school year? The track season was over, but he still had finals to give, papers to grade, end-of-the-year commitments. Surely he didn't need any more to do.

She tugged the shirt into place. Luke probably thought they'd meet a time or two, talk about some ideas, and then let someone else do the work.

But the committee members were the ones who would be doing the legwork. She could make phone calls during lulls in her business day, but she knew from Mandy that teachers didn't have the same freedom. The phones usually weren't available during their one planning period and the rest of the day was spent in the classroom.

After Sam's surprise motion and the immediate approval by the rest of the committee, she had been too stunned to do much more than agree when Helen suggested that the committee meet sometime during the next week so they could bring a preliminary report back to the next DBC meeting. The others on the committee had decided on Thursday evening, since that seemed the most open evening of the week for everyone involved. A few more announcements, a motion to adjourn, and the meeting had been over.

Luke had disappeared before she could talk to him. He didn't understand what was involved, she thought as she braided her hair. She would go to the high school on Monday and explain, in detail, what needed to be done. Once Luke understood the extent of the work, he would be more than happy to bow out.

The Founders Day Event was to be a major fund-raiser for the downtown group. They hoped to both create interest in the downtown and raise enough funds to start a major advertising campaign. And if money was available, they could start the beautification process that Coach Green had mentioned.

She locked the front door and walked down the front steps to her car, her mood lightened by her decision. Luke would be grateful once he realized how much time she was saving him. Their relationship would shift into that of friends and she could be rid of this annoying habit she had of feeling so young whenever she was around him.

A spring breeze danced around her legs and she inhaled deeply, taking in the fresh scent of her mother's early roses. She'd tell her mother how they were doing when she made her weekly phone call.

Her brow wrinkled as she tried to remember where her parents were. Since Tessa's graduation from high school, her mother had traveled with her father on his trucking runs. Every Friday, unless they were home, Tessa called and let them know about her week and they gave her news from their end.

They were supposed to be in the Pacific Northwest. She grinned. If they were near Seattle, then they would see her great-aunt. Which meant at least another box of goodies for her shop.

When she arrived at the Reynolds house, Anna opened the door before Tessa could even ring the bell. "Hi, Tessa."

"Hi, Anna." Tessa leaned down and gave the little girl a big hug. "Jake and Christine ready to go?"

Anna grabbed Tessa's hand and dragged her into the living room. "I don't know. She's been throwing up all day," Anna confessed in a low whisper. "I don't think she should go anywhere. She should just go to bed and rest."

Tessa bit the inside of her cheek to stop from grinning at the seven-year-old's grownup tone. She bent down until she was even with Anna's ear. "Maybe she just needs to get away for a little bit. Get her mind off how she feels."

"Secrets?"

Tessa straightened so quickly, she thought her back would crack. "Luke?"

"Hi." He slowly folded the newspaper he was holding and got to his feet, dropping the paper into a rack next to the sofa. "I heard you were coming over."

"Oh, really?" *Oh, that was clever,* she thought, wishing she could follow Christine's advice and just ignore him. *He's just another friend,* she reminded herself. *Treat him like you would any other friend.*

"Yeah, Jake and I were planning to finish some work in the basement tonight."

"Oh, I didn't think about Jake's plans. . . ." She chewed on her lower lip and then shook her head. "The basement can wait. Christine needs to get out of the house."

Luke nodded. "I agree." He glanced over to where Anna was coloring at a low table, and dropped his voice another notch. "Christine doesn't even know that's why I came over. Jake caught me as soon as I drove up and told me you were coming over to baby-sit. I would have left right then but Christine saw me so I told her I had just stopped by to see how she was. I offered to keep Anna company until you got here so they could get ready in peace."

Tessa barely stopped her mouth from dropping open. "You agree with me?"

He grinned, lines crinkling around his eyes. "Amazing, isn't it? We should probably watch that the floor doesn't open up and swallow us."

"Why would the floor open up?" Anna asked in her piping little voice from across the room. She bent down and ran a finger over the smooth wood. "Jake did a good job on this floor."

Luke chuckled. "It's an expression, punkin. It means something very surprising just happened."

"You can say that again," Tessa murmured.

He caught her eye and she blinked at his expression. If she didn't have a lifetime of experience behind her, she would almost think that Luke was flirting with her. But friends didn't flirt. And she was determined to be friends with him.

Which reminded her of the meeting last night.

"Luke, about the committee—"

"Little pitchers have big ears," he murmured.

She frowned at him. "What?"

He jerked his head toward Anna. "Do you want to have this argument right now?"

Her earlier charitable mood toward him vanished. "I am *not* having an argument with you. I just think we need to talk about last night."

He grinned. "Sounds like the start of an argument to me."

She exhaled a long breath and mentally counted to ten. She didn't argue with her other friends. She would not start with him. "Luke, listen, I don't know if you realize the amount of work involved—"

"We're ready." Christine entered the living room. "Oh, hi, Tessa. I didn't know you were here."

Tessa turned away from Luke and gave her friend a bright smile. "I just arrived a few minutes ago."

"Luke thinks the floor is going to swallow her up," Anna said, dropping her crayons and racing across the room to Christine's side.

Christine's eyes narrowed. "Swallow her up?"

"And he said something about little pitchers and big ears." She frowned. "I think he was talking about a ball game but I don't think it's nice to say someone has big ears."

From behind her, she could hear Luke's snort of laughter. Tessa groaned. "She misunderstood something Luke said," she said.

Jake strode into the room from the kitchen, a broad grin on his handsome face as he stopped next to Tessa. "Do we need to separate you children?"

They had sounded like a couple of squabbling children. Tessa gave Jake a rueful grin. "No, 'Daddy,' we'll be good. Did you find a movie to see?"

Christine nodded. "It starts in about twenty minutes, so

we'll need to run." She grabbed both of Tessa's hands. "You're sure you didn't have anything else to do?"

Tessa squeezed Christine's fingers gently. "I'm positive. Now go on, forget about everything except having a good time. You need to relax. Didn't Greg say that was the best thing you could do for the baby?"

Christine nodded. "I'm trying. But every time I settle down, my stomach gets a little active."

Jake wrapped his arm around her shoulders. "Come on, you heard Tessa. We're going to be wild and fancy-free tonight." He led her toward the front door and tugged it open. "Listen to Tessa," he told Anna, bending down to give her a kiss on the cheek. "We'll sneak in and kiss you good-night when we get back."

Anna shut the door behind them and came back to Tessa. Luke still stood next to the couch. "I didn't have supper yet," Anna announced in a loud voice.

Tessa nodded and started for the kitchen. "I know. I told Christine we would have something together."

"I like pizza."

"Do you?" Tessa pushed open the swinging door. "I bet Christine has something we can eat right here."

"I could pick up a pizza," Luke offered.

She glanced over her shoulder. He stood in the doorway of the kitchen, his shoulder propping the swinging door open.

She could understand why so many of her female friends saw him as an eligible bachelor. The ceiling light reflected on his hair, burnishing it a deep golden brown. He was the only Hunter child not to have inherited their mother's red hair. Except for his tall, lanky build, a replica of his father's, a stranger might be excused for not seeing any resemblance between Luke and the rest of his family. If she had been looking for a man in her life, she could almost see falling for him herself.

Good thing she wasn't looking.

She opened the refrigerator, studying the contents. "I thought you were just staying until I got here."

"I haven't eaten either. I thought maybe you could take pity on a hungry, single man. And I would be happy to get a pizza for us."

"I can cook something faster than we could get a pizza. But if you want a pizza, go ahead and get yourself one." She kept her head down, hoping he would take her hint and leave.

"You can eat with us, Uncle Luke, can't he, Tessa? Stay, please!"

Tessa glanced at him over the refrigerator door. "Uncle Luke?"

He shrugged. "She needed some sort of relationship for me. And since Jake and Christine have started adoption proceedings, it seemed natural."

She picked up a carton of eggs and closed the door. "I didn't know they were doing that." When *was* the last time she had really talked with Christine?

"They want to be my mom and dad." Anna clambered up on a stool next to the counter. "That way nobody can ever take me away from them."

Tessa's heart ached for the little girl. She missed her parents when they were on the road and she was an adult. She couldn't imagine being a little girl and losing her parents in a car crash and then coming to live with an older brother she had barely met. Except for some isolated incidents at school, Anna seemed to be adapting well, but Tessa guessed it would be a constant challenge. Knowing she had a permanent place in their family would probably help Anna adjust easier.

"So, what are we having?" Luke asked.

"Anna and I are having omelets." She dislodged a frying pan from the stack of pans under the counter.

"Uncle Luke can have one, too." Anna propped her elbows on the counter, her pointed little chin resting on her hands.

"Then Uncle Luke needs to help," Tessa said, knowing it was useless to argue with the little girl. And he didn't seem to be in any hurry to leave.

"Okay." He washed his hands in the sink. "What do I do first?"

She directed him to chop the tomatoes and fresh mushrooms she had seen in the bottom of the refrigerator. As she whipped the eggs, she asked Anna about school. Pouring the mixture gently into the frying pan, she could hear Luke softly whistling under his breath as he chopped the vegetables.

She would never have imagined cooking dinner with Luke complacently helping her while she listened to a child tell about her day at school. Almost like an ordinary couple, she thought. The irony of the situation forced a chuckle out of her.

Anna paused in her story about the difficult art project they had done that day and frowned. "It's not a funny story, Tessa."

Tessa bent down and kissed Anna's nose. "I'm not laughing at you," she explained. "You just made me think of a funny thought."

The chopping stopped behind her. She knew Luke was watching them. She couldn't look at him with the image of them as a couple so clear in her mind. Not that she would ever seriously consider such a thing. Somehow, though, Luke always seemed to know what she was thinking and she didn't want him to laugh at her. The idea might be preposterous but she didn't need him to confirm it.

By the time they had eaten dinner, finished the dishes, and played three games of Candyland, Anna was yawning and rubbing her eyes. Luke had ignored all of Tessa's hints to go home and she had finally decided that it was pleasant sharing the responsibility of watching Anna with him. He had played the game with more patience than she was able to muster, reminding Anna several times of the real rules of the game and still managing to let her reach the end first.

"Anna, you need to go to bed." He positioned the lid on the game box and carried it back to the shelf in the family room.

"I'm not tired." Her argument lost some weight as her last word was swallowed by another yawn.

"Not a bit?" he asked, squatting down in front of her.

She shook her head, her eyes wide. "See? I'm not tired at all."

"Hmmm." He tipped his head to one side and studied her face.

"What?" She blinked a long, slow blink, and Tessa bit her lips to keep from grinning.

"I think you're right." He glanced at Tessa over Anna's head and gave her a quick wink.

Her stomach fluttered and then settled down. He wasn't flirting with her. He just wanted her to go along with his game.

Not that she was sure of her part. Somehow, he planned to convince Anna she was tired. But what was she supposed to do?

"You know, I bet you don't need any sleep at all tonight."

Anna nodded. "I don't. I could stay up all the way till morning and still play tomorrow."

"I bet you could." Luke hid a big yawn behind his hand. "Now, me, I need some sleep. I had a long day at school today."

Tessa caught on. Her pretend yawn quickly turned into a real one. After the meeting last night she had found it hard to settle for the night and her short night was catching up with her. "Me, too. Not at school, of course," she said with a smile at Anna. "But working at the shop wore me out."

Anna's glance swung from one to the other. "I had to work at school, too, you know."

Tessa nodded. "I know. You told me about it while we were cooking."

"I didn't even tell you everything." Anna yawned again and this time rubbed her eyes. "We had a whole lot of work this morning." Another yawn escaped her little mouth.

"Christine said you've been working really hard."

Anna nodded, her eyelids drooping halfway over her eyes. "Maybe I should go to bed. The nurse came in the other day and said we have to give our bodies and brains rest every day."

"Not a bad idea." Luke shifted until his back was to her. "Would you like a piggyback ride to your room?"

Anna grinned and climbed onto his back. Her arms wrapped around his neck, she giggled as he bounced her down the hallway to her room.

I just hope she doesn't get a second wind, Tessa thought, following them. Luke deposited Anna with a plop on the bed. "There you go."

She popped to her feet, her hands raised toward his neck. "I need a good-night kiss," she begged.

He bent down and rubbed his whiskery cheek against her soft one. "Ouch, ouch, ouch!" she shrieked. Tessa stepped forward in alarm and then recognized the cries as teasing ones.

"Good night." Luke disengaged her little arms from around his neck and gave her a quick kiss on the nose. "I'll see you later. Thanks for inviting me for supper."

He left the room and Tessa breathed a sigh of relief. Watching him with Anna brought out a side of him she had never seen before. Even though he drove her crazy, she felt more comfortable with the Luke who teased her and called her munchkin. This other Luke was a stranger to her and she didn't want to think of him as the kind of man who cared about children and came up with silly games for them. That Luke would be harder to ignore or even treat as a friend.

She helped Anna change into her pajamas and then waited while she brushed her teeth. The burst of energy she had shown with Luke was disappearing and she could barely hold up her hand to wash her face.

Tessa took the warm cloth from her hand. "Let me help." She ran the rag around the little nose and cheeks and then patted her face dry. "Come on, I'll carry you to bed."

Anna nuzzled into Tessa's shoulder, her arms wrapped around her neck. Holding Anna's small frame against her hip, Tessa carried her into the room and gently lowered her onto the bed, tucking the covers around her shoulders.

"I need to say prayers," Anna murmured.

Tessa settled on the edge of the bed, listening as Anna thanked God for the day and for her friends and her family, itemizing each one. "And thank you for Tessa and Luke making me supper," she added. "Amen."

A warm glow spread through Tessa. She didn't know if anyone except her parents included her in their daily prayers. It didn't even matter that she had been lumped in with Luke.

Tucking a strand of hair behind Anna's ears, Tessa sat by the side of the bed and rubbed Anna's back until the little girl's breathing slowed to a rhythmic pace. Clicking off the bedside light, she tiptoed out of the room and down the hall.

Her thoughts still on the pleasure of tucking a sleepy girl into bed, she didn't see Luke until she practically stepped on his toes. She gasped and jumped sideways, stumbling and catching herself by grabbing his arms.

His hands caught her under the elbows, steadying her. She took a deep breath and tried to press a hand to her chest but his fingers were still locked around her arms.

"You can let go now," she said.

He grinned. "I like having you trapped like this."

She slid out of his grasp and took a step backward, stopping when she bumped against a low end table. "Very funny." She rubbed her hands over the skin that he had touched. He hadn't hurt her but her arms still felt the imprint of his fingers. "What are you doing here? I thought you left after you told Anna good night."

He shrugged. "I don't have a key so I didn't know how I could lock you in."

She stared at him in disbelief. "I think we'd be safe for a few minutes with the house unlocked. It's not like we live in the city or anything."

"Maybe we don't but it's not a smart thing to leave your

house unlocked at night." He scowled at her. "You don't leave your house unlocked, do you?"

She shook her head. "No. But couldn't you have pushed in the bottom button and pulled the door shut behind you?"

She walked over to the door to check. Satisfied that he could have left them locked in that way, she turned around and bumped into his solid chest.

"Why are you trying so hard to get rid of me?" he asked softly, his hands cupping her elbows again.

"I—" She swallowed, her words stuck in her throat. Why was she? The evening had been enjoyable, a welcome change from her quiet evenings alone at home.

Not that she had ever thought about being alone with Luke. "It's just—" She tried again. "We don't both have to wait for Christine and Jake."

"I don't mind. Do you have somewhere you need to go?"

He hadn't released her arms. She found it difficult to breathe and told herself it was because he was blocking her air. "No. I just . . ."

"What?"

She lifted her head and found herself looking directly at his mouth. She licked suddenly dry lips. If she moved just an inch closer . . .

She didn't get to finish the thought. The door opened behind her and Luke tugged her out of the way before the knob rammed into her back. She took a moment to gather her thoughts before she turned around and met Christine and Jake's surprised looks.

"Hi." She knew she sounded overly cheerful but she couldn't stop herself.

Had she seriously been considering kissing Luke? He was her best friend's brother!

She didn't know what she said to Christine or Jake or

what they said to her. Her only desire was to get out of their house and back to the safety of her own before she disgraced herself. She couldn't bring herself to look at Luke, afraid of what she would see in his eyes. Brushing off Christine's thanks, she excused herself and raced to her car, driving away without a glance into her rearview mirror to see if Luke had followed her.

Crawling under her covers, she pressed her hands against flaming cheeks. *Oh, please, please don't let him know what I was thinking,* she prayed. It was just a goofy, spur-of-the-moment, idle thought.

Her fevered thoughts cooled and she rolled onto her back, staring at the shadows of the leaves from outside as they danced over the ceiling. Her mind drifted to a memory of just before she left for college.

Luke was home, having graduated from college that spring. He had been hired to replace Coach Green at the high school and his parents had thrown a party to celebrate his graduation and his new job. She had gone with Abby and Mandy, meeting Christine there, all of them thrilled with their new status as high school graduates and feeling very grownup.

Sometime during the evening, she had wandered outside, finding a quiet spot in the Hunters' backyard. College loomed as an exciting adventure but she was also finding the thought of being away from her friends and family frightening. Graduation, the imminent departure for college, her mother's announcement that she would be traveling with her father, had all hit her with a thud and she had struggled to maintain the excited facade that her friends seemed to exhibit with no trouble. With her mother's decision, she had even had the security of coming home on the weekends to her family taken away.

A full moon had lighted her path as she made her way to a bench in the far corner of the garden. Sitting there, she had reminded herself that she would do fine, that she was capable of anything, that college wasn't forever. She had been in the midst of consoling herself when she had heard footsteps and looked up to see Luke standing in front of her.

"What are you doing here?" His voice was low, as if he didn't want to disturb her.

"Just taking a breather." She forced herself to smile. "What are you doing? Shouldn't the guest of honor be inside?"

"I got tired of repeating myself." He sat down next to her and she scooted away to give him more room. "I don't know how they think I can tell them what's going to happen when I haven't even started my job yet."

"Maybe they expect you to predict the future now that you have a college degree."

His smile glinted in the moonlight. "You think college gives you magical powers?"

She shook her head. "I don't think so. But a lot of the people in there never went to college. And you are the closest thing we have to a celebrity."

"Next year, somebody else will win the state championship."

"But you've put Durant on the map. We're in the history books."

He turned around until he was facing her. "What history books?"

"You know what I mean. Why do you always have to argue with everything I say?"

He laughed. "This from the girl who would tell me it was daytime if I told her it was night."

She tilted her chin up. "That's not true."

"I didn't come out here to argue with you."

His eyes were hidden in the dark and for a moment, she wondered what it would be like to kiss him. Not that he had ever acted like he was interested. But sitting together in the moonlight, both older . . .

He shifted his position and the moment passed. They had sat for a few minutes in the quiet garden, both lost in their own thoughts. The silence hadn't been threatening and she had been pleased he didn't expect her to talk to him.

Just before he went inside, he had asked her if she was excited about going to college. She had been tempted to tell him about her fears, certain he would understand but she had suddenly felt shy. She didn't know this new Luke. With all the other changes, she didn't think she could handle one more.

When he went inside, she had waited, reluctant to go in right after him as if they had been meeting outside. Once she made her way into the house, he had given her his lopsided grin and then ignored her as he had the rest of the evening, just as if nothing had ever happened between them outside in the dark. She had gone off to college confident that at least some things never changed.

She frowned, her thoughts coming back to the present. Except for that one night, she had never thought about kissing Luke. He had been a thorn in her side, a pebble in her shoe, a constant irritation that had been part of her life since she was five years old.

But as she drifted off to sleep, her contrary brain wondered what it would be like to have his lips against hers.

Chapter Three

By the light of day, her musings about Luke seemed nothing more than a tired mind floundering around before settling for the night. Working in her office relaxed her and she was able to push the thoughts to the back of her mind. She was pleased with the shop and the reputation she was already earning, after only two years of being open.

She sorted through the small stack of papers on her desk. "Fern, do you have that order for Mrs. Higgins?" she called toward the main room of the shop.

The beaded curtain that separated the office from the display room rustled and a slight woman several decades older than Tessa came into the room. "I think I filed it," she said, opening the top drawer of the large cabinet against the wall. "I thought we were done."

"We were. She just had a question about the nightstand and I thought I would check the order form."

Fern handed her the slip of paper and after Tessa's

thanks, she went back into the main room. Tessa tossed her braid over her shoulder with a distracted motion and made a notation on the yellow pad of paper in front of her. Soft music from the stereo system next to her floated around the office and into the display room. She hummed under her breath, flipping pages and writing down notes as she worked.

Only a few more weeks were left in the school year and then her busiest time would start. Tourists visiting the Ozarks often wandered off the regular path and into Durant. Her hope was that with the committee working together, they could entice people to plan to visit, rather than just straggling in.

The day had been slow, with only a few customers coming in and most of those only to browse. A few parents had wandered in to find gifts for their children's teachers and she had made a note to look for suitable small items when she went to auctions. Finding the right present was the motto of her shop and she prided herself on her selections. If she could convince people that she had what they needed or could find something in a relatively short time, they wouldn't travel to other communities to buy their gift items.

The curtain rattled again. "Tessa, if it's okay, I'm going home."

Tessa stretched, brushing a loose curl behind her ear, and glanced at the clock. "I didn't realize it was so late." She waved a hand toward the dwindling pile of papers in front of her. "I'll just finish these last forms and go myself."

Fern picked up her purse and coat. "Good. You do remember I won't be in on Monday? I'm going to my granddaughter's award ceremony."

Tessa had forgotten the actual date but she did remember

Fern mentioning she needed time off during the next week. Working by herself on Monday would mean she couldn't see Luke then, but she could easily slip off on one of the other days for a little bit to talk to him about the committee before they met on Thursday.

She picked up a small music box from a low shelf. "What do you think?"

"Oh, it's lovely!" Fern turned it around several times before extending the box toward Tessa.

"It's yours," Tessa said, locking her hands behind her back.

Fern's mouth widened into an O. "Tessa, I can't take this."

"It's not for you exactly," Tessa said. "It's a present for Julie. When I saw it, I knew it would be perfect for her. A bonus from me to you that you can share with her. I would never get anything done if you weren't here to help."

Fern traced the delicate design on the top with a gentle finger. "Are you sure?"

"I'm positive." Tessa stood up, arching her shoulders before she gave the older woman a hug. "Now, go on."

She followed Fern to the front door and waved her goodbye. As she turned toward her office, she felt the familiar tug of ownership. She had created this. She had turned a worn-out building into Treasure Seekers' Haven, a place that invited browsing and encouraged purchasing. She trailed her fingers over the walnut buffet sitting in front of the wide window and twitched the skirt of the china doll arrayed neatly on top. A display of porcelain dishes caught her eye and she shifted one of the saucers so that it was centered more attractively.

The bell tingled on the door and she glanced over her

shoulder. Her welcoming smile wavered when she saw the man who entered.

"Hello, Mr. Owens."

"Tessa."

The solid man advanced into the room, a wide smile on his broad face. He ran a hand through his thinning hair and then used the same hand to pat her on the shoulder.

She forced back a desire to flinch. He had always patted the heads of the children who came into his shop for sweets. Now that she was older, and taller, he had taken to patting her shoulder and she had to use all her willpower not to pull away. She didn't think he meant it disrespectfully but she noticed he didn't pat any of the other storeowners in that same condescending way.

"What can I do for you?" She folded her arms over her chest, smiling at him as she would any potential customer.

"It's about the Founders Day Festival."

Her pulse quickened. If he was willing to talk to her about the festival, it could only mean that he accepted her as a colleague. "Yes?" she asked softly.

"I was thinking about what happened at the meeting the other night."

"Oh?"

He opened his mouth but instead of any words, he let out a loud sneeze. Shaking his head, he took out a large handkerchief from his jacket pocket, blowing his nose and carefully refolding the handkerchief before putting it back in his pocket. She waited, knowing that if she said anything at all, even "Gesundheit," he would launch into a description of the pollen count and how difficult his allergies had been recently.

"I'm a little worried about that letter Luke Hunter read," he continued.

"It shouldn't be a problem. We planned the Founders Day Festival even before we discovered the town was a hundred years old."

"That's just it."

Tessa stared at him. "What's just it?"

"If the town isn't a hundred years old until next year, we should wait and have the festival then. It would give us more time to prepare, advertise. And then we would really be honoring the founders of our town."

Tessa forced her lips to curve upward. "Mr. Owens, the festival isn't just about remembering the founders of Durant. I mean it is, but it's also to help the downtown. If we wait another year—"

"I just think we should," he interrupted. "Otherwise, how do we advertise?"

"As a celebration of our heritage. We can do that anytime." She gave him the smile she used with shoppers who were almost ready to purchase an item. "The people won't mind that we're a year or two off. In fact, most of them won't even notice, especially if we don't say anything. We'll just celebrate the town's beginning and not even mention the year."

He didn't look entirely convinced. "You think it could work?"

"I do." She led the way toward her front door. "This will be good for business, Mr. Owens. You'll see."

He gave her a distracted nod and walked out the door. She watched him head toward his own shop, and then dropped into a low bench that she had painstakingly refinished after finding it covered under layers of thick, dark paint.

She was right, wasn't she? A number of the surrounding communities had yearly celebrations that had little to do with their beginnings. Instead, they had chosen a theme unique to their area and developed an event that drew in hundreds, sometimes thousands, of people. She had been thinking of those when she had suggested the Founders Day festival, intending to go back in time for ideas. The year of Durant's beginning hadn't even been part of her original plan.

She stiffened her shoulders and stood up, locking the door and flipping the sign to CLOSED before she went back to the office. They could go in any direction. No publicity had been done yet. The idea was still in the planning stages. If others had the same concerns that Mr. Owens had expressed, maybe it would be better to look for a different angle.

Sunday crawled by. She saw several friends at church in the morning and smilingly refused their dinner invitations. She felt restless and didn't want to inflict her contrary mood on anyone else.

She moved furniture in the living room and stripped off the last of the old wallpaper. Since her parents had started to travel, they had turned the house over to her and she had been systematically redoing the different rooms. Her bedroom had been the first one she tackled, giving her a chance to experiment, and then she had done the upstairs bathroom. With the shop requiring less physical labor, she had decided to start on the living room.

By the time she dropped into bed that night, she was too tired to think, let alone dream. She woke up Monday morning refreshed and eager to go to work alone for a few hours in her shop, her mind free of any worries about the committee or Luke.

Gary Templar, a local lawyer, stopped by around noon

and invited her to lunch. She eagerly accepted, knowing that she would enjoy an hour of light conversation with a handsome man who hadn't known her since childhood. They had met several weeks earlier when Gary moved into an office building across the way from her shop. She had welcomed him to the community and invited him to join the DBC. He had declined, stating that he was only leasing the building.

"So, what happened at the meeting?" he asked after they ordered sandwiches at the fast-food restaurant on the edge of town. The café had been too busy for the short time he had available.

"Not much. We're going ahead with the planning for the Founders Day Festival even though it turns out the town probably isn't one hundred years old this year." She frowned, remembering how Luke's news had stifled her excitement.

"What's the matter?"

She hesitated, not sure how to tell him about Luke's involvement with the committee without sounding like she was whining. She still couldn't understand why he was interested in being so involved. "Most of the ideas I had were for the one-hundred-year theme," she said.

"So you come up with new ideas. That shouldn't be a problem for you." His smile lit up his dark eyes and she felt a warm glow flow through her.

Her good mood lasted until midmorning Tuesday. Fern was already in the shop when Tessa arrived, her head feeling thick and heavy. A storm had broken in the night and the branches scratching against her bedroom window had awakened her just before the lightning and thunder did. When she couldn't get to sleep right away, she had crawled downstairs and paid bills instead.

"Good morning," Fern chirped, handing her a cup of tea.

" 'Morning." Tessa sipped the tea gratefully, the warm liquid easing down her throat.

"That was quite a storm last night, wasn't it?"

Tessa marveled at her elderly assistant's cheerful mood. Widowed two years earlier, Fern had applied for the job of assistant as soon as the sign was posted in the window. At first Tessa had been worried that Fern was too quiet and shy, but that soon turned out to be a blessing. She didn't like a lot of chattering herself and when Fern did talk, she had something important to say. With her parents away much of the time, Tessa found it comforting to have someone around who could give her advice if needed.

Today, a little peace and quiet would have been appreciated.

"That was a storm," Tessa agreed, unable to think of any other comment.

"I gathered together the items for the new window display," Fern continued, picking up her own teacup and carrying it over to the small sink in the office.

"Great." Tessa drained the last of her tea and gave her assistant a small smile. Her headache wasn't completely gone but it did seem to be dwindling.

Fifteen minutes later, she felt more her normal self. Working in the store always improved her disposition. "How was the awards ceremony?" Tessa asked as they carried a narrow bench toward the window display at the front of the store.

"Very nice. Julie received a scholarship from our women's group and I presented the award. She was thrilled."

They settled the bench in the middle of the display window. "That was special," Tessa said, arranging a quilted shawl over the back of the bench. "She's worked hard over the last few years."

"I know. It will be so strange, though, to have her go away. I've seen her at least twice a week since the day she was born."

Tessa added a cobalt-blue glass vase to the small table beside the bench, fluffing the silk columbines until the flowers almost looked real. "She'll be back," she promised. "She won't forget her grandma or her town."

"I know it." Fern sighed. "It just won't be the same."

Tessa thought about that as she wrote the checks for the monthly bills. Durant was not the same town she had known as a little girl. People had grown up, moved away, died. When Mandy had moved to Kansas City, their group of four had seemed splintered, broken. Even though they still all got together and visited, it wasn't the same.

"Because they're all married," she murmured, her pen poised above the checkbook.

"Did you say something?" Fern called from the front of the shop.

"No, just talking to myself," she called back.

She dropped the pen on her desk and propped her elbows on either side of the book, resting her chin on her hands. How had it happened? Not that anyone had been surprised when Abby married Tim. They had met when he moved to town during their eighth-grade year, and neither one had looked at anyone else after that.

Christine hadn't been a surprise, either. Her choice of husband had taken everyone unawares but Christine's desire to be married and raise a family had been a regular part of their teenage conversations. While Abby had known whom she was going to marry, Christine's future husband had been more nebulous. Seeing her with Jake, though, Tessa knew that she had found the right man.

And Mandy . . . Tessa grinned and shook her head. Mandy had sworn she wouldn't return to Durant, that she wanted nothing but the city life. Tessa had always felt she protested too much and when her grandmother was sick, she hadn't been startled to find Mandy rushing back to care for Rebecca Powell. Granny Becca held a special place in the hearts of all four of the girls, fixing them delicious snacks when they stayed over, teaching them card games that had kept them up all night.

A twinge of guilt stabbed her. She hadn't known about Granny Becca's health condition until her doctor called Mandy home. *I should have visited more,* Tessa thought.

But the shop had taken all of her time. Her dream to have her own business had started the day her high school business teacher had suggested she attend an estate auction for an extra-credit project. Standing in the middle of the collection, excitement had rushed through her. She had felt the history of the elderly couple, seen their life portrayed through the belongings that they had shared, recognized the beauty they created together.

She wanted to help others find the perfect items for their own homes. Her mother and father had spent little time or money on their house, choosing furniture more for practicality than longevity. Since they had turned the house over to her, she had been replacing the nondescript pieces with ones that had more character.

She shook her head and picked up the pen, signing her name with a flourish before ripping the check out of the book and sliding it into its envelope. Stretching, she stood up and gathered the stack of bills.

"I'm going to the post office," she informed Fern. "Hold the fort."

A breeze drifted over her face as she walked out of the shop, a tiny infant cousin to the wind that had blown through town last night. The sky was a perfect blue, not a cloud in sight. The sound of a mower floated lightly on the air and she inhaled deeply, taking in the scent of the rain that had sprinkled the town last night and the aroma of newly cut grass.

Rounding the corner, she waved at an acquaintance driving past and waited for the single stoplight to change before crossing the street. The stone front of the post office sat proudly between two brick buildings and she ran her finger over the marker stating that the building was an historical part of the community.

She ran up the steps, pausing at the top to survey the rest of the town. The post office, hospital, and a bank building towered over the rest of the buildings. An apartment building sat next to the fire station and its windows opened onto the fire station roof. She could see two people sitting on chaise lounges on its roof and she waved, getting an answering wave back.

A feeling of contentment swept through her. This was her town. Whatever it took, she would help the downtown grow.

"Hi, Tessa." The postal clerk smiled at her as she came into the room.

"Hi, Tom." She moved around the sign that said WAIT HERE FOR NEXT AVAILABLE CLERK and approached the window. "I need another roll of stamps."

"No problem." He opened his drawer and pulled out a roll, punching in the amount on his keyboard. "I heard I missed an interesting meeting the other night."

She glanced at him, confused for a moment, and then remembered that Sam had mentioned that Tom was also part owner of the Sports Shack. "Nothing too outrageous," she said carefully. She handed him the money for the stamps and then peeled one off, sticking it on the top envelope. "What did you hear?"

"Just that there's some debate about whether we'll have the Festival this year or not."

Mr. Owens, she thought. "I don't think that's an issue. We need a fund-raiser."

He nodded. "I know. If we don't do something soon, downtown is going to die."

She was glad to hear someone voice the same opinion. She stuck a stamp on the last envelope and handed him the pile. "You need to come to the meetings and let everybody hear that. I don't think some of them understand what's happening."

He dropped the envelopes in the basket behind him. "I plan to be there next week. I would have been there last week, but—"

"Oh, Tom, I'm sorry," she broke in. "How is the baby?"

He grinned. "Fine, she just had a really bad cough. But Kelly had been up all the night before and I didn't feel right leaving her alone." He dug out his wallet. "You want to see a new picture?"

She admired Kaylee's latest picture and then made her escape. She didn't mind looking at baby pictures but recently, it seemed like everyone she knew had pictures of their children and she was spending a lot of time looking at them.

"Which is okay," she muttered out loud. "Your biological clock is nowhere near the end of its time."

The image of a clock in her mind, she glanced at her

watch. School would be just about over. If she hurried, she could catch Luke before he went home and talk to him right now.

She walked through the crowd of high school students rushing through the long hallway, noting they seemed noisier than she remembered. She grinned. *Probably because you were usually in the thick of the noise,* she reminded herself.

She paused halfway down a hallway, trying to get her bearings.

"You looking for someone?"

She hesitated a moment more and then turned toward the voice. Students lingered by the lockers and she couldn't tell who had spoken to her. "Coach Hunter," she said finally.

A gangly youth broke away from a small group of boys and loped toward her. "He's probably in his office, by the P.E. classes."

"Thanks."

He caught up with her. "You want me to show you the way?"

She bit back a sigh. No, she wanted to be back in her shop, but her mother had drilled it into her that you never put off an unpleasant task. "Don't you want to go home?" she asked politely, hoping he would take the hint and go away. She didn't need any witnesses to her visit.

"Nah, I'm in no hurry." He held a door open for her at the end of the hall and waited until it closed behind them before adding, "Besides, I don't have much to do once I get there. At least, until I have to go to work tonight."

"I see."

They walked down a narrow set of steps. The air changed, bringing with it the scent of chlorine and high school lockers. "You know Coach Hunter well?" he asked, leading her toward a small hallway.

"I'm friends with his sister."

She glanced at the boy and saw that he was watching her with a shy smile and an intent look in his eyes. She recognized the signs. His teenage hormones on full alert, he was reacting to her male to female.

The notion dispelled part of her anxiety about confronting Luke. Feeling more confident, she straightened her shoulders and followed him until he stopped outside a partially opened door.

"Hey, Coach Hunter, somebody to see ya." He leaned inside the door, his hand wrapped around the doorjamb. "And she's a real looker," he whispered in a loud voice.

"Thanks, Matt."

A chair scraped across the wooden floor and then the door opened wider. Luke stopped in the doorway, a clipboard in his hand, and stared at her in confusion. "Tessa?"

"Hi." She tipped her chin up a little higher.

"She said she was looking for you, so I brought her down," Matt offered.

"Thanks." Luke swung away from Tessa and frowned at the boy standing between them. The fluorescent ceiling light sparkled on Luke's hair, bringing out red highlights she'd never noticed before. "Not the way to announce somebody."

"She couldn't hear me," Matt grumbled. He gave Tessa a quick glance, his eyes wide, his Adam's apple prominent as he swallowed. "You couldn't, could ya?"

She swallowed her grin, knowing exactly what he was referring to. But his expression reminded her of Christine's puppy just before he thought he was going to get in trouble and she decided to take pity on him. "I just heard you tell him that somebody was here to see him. Maybe not proper by most etiquette standards." She gave a shrug. "But it did the job, right?"

Relief flooded his eyes. "Yeah." He tucked his thumbs into his front pockets. "See ya, Coach. I work tonight if you want to come by." He jerked his head toward Tessa. "I'd fix you up real special," he added with a wide grin.

"That's twice," Luke said quietly. "One more and you're out."

"Then I better take off. 'Bye, ma'am." He saluted Tessa and sauntered off the way they had come.

"That wasn't very nice of you," she said to Luke as soon as she was certain Matt was out of earshot.

"Tessa, he's a student. And if you had any sense, you'd see he embarrassed you."

"Why? Because he thinks I look good?" She planted her fists on her hips, her eyes narrowed.

"He's a teenage boy. Any female over thirteen looks good." He turned around and headed back into his office.

The wind taken out of her sails, she followed him.

Papers covered the top of the battered wooden desk in the middle of the room. A large yearly calender covered one wall, many of the squares filled in with scrawled dates she knew represented track meets. A pile of running clothes, complete with two pairs of shoes, sat on a chair in the corner of the room and a sagging bookcase filled the wall nearest the door.

She hesitated inside the door. "I'm interrupting you." Now that she was facing him, she didn't know how to bring up her topic.

He glanced around the room and then gave her a wide grin that brought out a creased dimple in his cheek. "No, it usually looks this way. At least until school is out and I have to clean up so they can do the floors."

He scooped a stack of notebooks off a chair and dropped them on the floor. "Sit down."

Luke dropped the clipboard he had been holding on the stack of books that wobbled precariously at the edge of his desk and sat down in the chair behind his desk, crossing his arms over his chest. "So, what are you doing here? Didn't find out you failed a class and have to redo high school, did you?"

She pressed her lips together. "No."

He grinned. "A joke, munchkin. You graduated with honors, didn't you?"

"Yes," she said in surprise. "How did you remember that?"

"The graduating class always sits in order by grade point average. You sat by Christine."

"Of course." She didn't understand why she felt disappointed.

She took refuge in his other comment. "You know, Luke, I've grown up. I'm not a munchkin anymore."

He propped his elbows on the desk and rested his chin on his folded hands, surveying her carefully from head to toe. She held herself still, even though she wanted to wrap her arms around her middle. Why hadn't she kept her mouth shut?

"You're right," he said slowly, crinkles appearing at the corner of each eye. "Definitely not a munchkin."

A warm glow spread through her at the appreciation in his voice. Surely he wasn't just reacting to her with his hormones?

And why would you even care? she chided herself. *Chris-*

tine's brother, remember? Think of the disaster if things didn't work out.

His chair creaked as he leaned back and he braced his feet on a free corner of the desk. She focused on his face. "But I may have a hard time breaking the habit," he said. "I've called you munchkin for a long time. Now why don't you tell me the reason you left your shop?"

"No real reason . . ."

He raised a hand, halting her words. "Come on, Tessa, I've known you long enough. You never could tell a lie."

She huffed and crossed her arms over her chest. "I'm not lying."

He laughed. "See? You're not telling the truth even now. Your eyes get all smoky and your nose twitches."

She raised a hand to the offending item. "That's because it's so dusty in here."

"It might be. But you still can't tell a lie." He dropped his feet to the floor and stood up. "I'd love to sit here and chat, Tessa, but I do have work to do and I suppose you do, too."

He paused in front of her, his head tipped toward hers as he studied her face. "Are you going to tell me the real reason you came over?"

She schooled her features into a bland expression even as her stomach churned. Sitting this close to him, she didn't know how she could bring up the committee. But if she didn't, he would think she had just dropped by to see him.

Which was the farthest thing from the truth.

He was her best friend's brother. They could be considered friends of a sort, too, even though they hadn't seen each other much until recently. Besides, she wasn't ready to settle down. Her business took up too much of her time and she liked her independence. Gary made no demands on her and she enjoyed their friendly, noncommittal dates. They could talk, laugh, enjoy each other's company, and then go their separate ways. No ties, no messes.

Not that Luke seemed ready to settle down either. If anything, Luke seemed to be even more reluctant to date than she was. Probably knew what a catch he was considered to be, she thought. If he went out with anyone, she probably started talking about marriage before the appetizers were finished.

"Tessa?"

She shook away the fanciful images. This was her own fault. If she had voiced her thoughts that night, she wouldn't be sitting in his office trying to get rid of ideas like Luke dating other women. If she hadn't been so stunned, she could have tackled Luke after the meeting and talked to him then. Or she could have said something when they were both at Christine's house. Waiting this long, it would seem as if she wanted him to give up the position because she didn't feel comfortable working with him.

Which might have been the point once but wasn't now. After that strange moment at Christine's house, she didn't want him thinking that she was uncomfortable because she was attracted to him. She probably could be attracted to him if she let herself. But she wouldn't. She was known for her self-control.

She inhaled and exhaled slowly. "Okay, here it is," she said carefully.

Luke perched on his desk, his arms crossed over his chest. She swallowed and looked down at her feet for a moment and then back to his face. "I don't think we should chair the committee together."

"Why not?"

Why not? Because I don't like what's happening to me

whenever I'm around you. I'm starting to get crazy thoughts.

But she couldn't say any of this out loud. She fell back on their past. "You and I can't be in the same room for more than ten minutes without arguing. You've said it yourself. How can we possibly work on a committee and get anything done?"

He grinned. "You could always agree with me."

She would not be sidetracked. "Luke, this fund-raiser is going to take a lot of work and a lot of time. Hours on the phone tracking down vendors, supplies. Not everyone has that much time to spare."

There, she'd said it. He'd realize how involved the work would be and graciously resign.

"I thought this festival was your idea."

She nodded. "It was."

"So why would you want to give it up?"

She stared at him. "I don't want to give it up. I want you to resign."

"Me?"

She took a deep breath and released it slowly. She would have to be blunt. "Luke, you don't realize how much work this will involve. With the end of school activities, gradu- ation . . ." She lifted her hands. "Everybody will understand if you decide you shouldn't take the position."

"But I already did."

She recognized the firm tone in his voice. He had used that same tone whenever he would tell them to stay away from his things or to quit following him around. All teasing gone, they knew he meant business.

Why was he doing this? For some inexplicable reason, he wanted to be on the committee.

"Fine." She slung her purse over her shoulder and stood up. "Don't say I didn't warn you."

She paused at the doorway and regarded him carefully, wondering how much she could say. "This town means a lot to me, Luke, and this festival could really help the downtown. If you think you can just get by with a smile and a wink, you're wrong. You're going to have to work or you're history."

She cringed at the terrible pun but stood her ground. He didn't say anything. Confident she had made her point, she marched out of the door without waiting for him to answer.

Chapter Four

The phone was ringing as she pushed her key into the door and she raced across the kitchen floor, grabbing it with a breathless, "Hello?"

"Tessa?"

She kicked off her pumps and dropped into a kitchen chair. "Hi, Christine. You must have radar or really good spies. I just came in the door and I have to leave in about ten minutes or I'll be late for a meeting."

She rubbed her foot, wiggling the cramp out of her toes. If she hadn't stayed too long at the office wrestling with a stubborn bank balance, she could have had time to soak her feet for a few minutes. Now, she'd be lucky to grab a bite to eat before she had to dash out the door again.

"What meeting is it this time?" Christine asked.

"The Founders Day Planning committee. We're looking at different options." Tessa started to complain about co-chairing with Luke and remembered just in time that Christine was his sister. And what was she going to complain about anyway?

She was finding it difficult to concentrate on the festival, her mind whirling from one possibility to another, while she considered how to break the connection with Luke.

And she wasn't even sure that was really what she wanted anymore. After her visit to the high school, she had half-expected Luke to come around the shop or call her at home, upset that she had doubted his own loyalty to the town. She knew her last comment hadn't been entirely fair. Luke supported the town through his teaching and the commitment he gave to the track team. Being on the committee could be just one more facet of his support.

They chatted a few more minutes before Tessa excused herself. She threw together a sandwich, gobbled it down, and then raced out the door.

Once in the small building that housed the town offices, she hurried down the tiled hallway and into the conference room. She halted a moment in the dark hallway and then clicked on the lights, glancing around, but the room was empty.

She waited fifteen minutes, her foot tapping an impatient rhythm on the floor. Her notes lay in front of her, a tentative agenda and timetable at five of the closest places.

By 7:30, she was certain no one was going to arrive. Disappointed and surprised at the lack of support, she gathered up her notes, stuffed everything back into her briefcase, and rose from her chair. Halfway across the room, she heard hurried footsteps racing down the hall.

Luke burst into the room. "Tessa!"

"Glad you could make it," she informed him icily. She moved past him but he stopped her with a hand on her arm.

"Make it? Make what?" He glanced around the room. "Have you been here since seven o'clock?"

She nodded. "We did have a meeting scheduled."

"Not here."

Her eyes widened. "What?"

He blew out a burst of warm air that fluttered a loose curl by her ear. "The meeting was at Bessie's house. She thought we'd think better in someone's living room than here. She also offered to make snacks," he said with a wide grin.

She stared at him, her fingers clenching on the handle of her briefcase. "Bessie? I didn't know she was on the committee." She vaguely remembered the older woman talking to them at the end of the meeting but everything had been in such a jumble.

"She volunteered last week. I thought she would be a great addition since she knows so much about the food industry."

Bessie's Café sold the best doughnuts in town and also kept the locals fed at breakfast and lunchtime. The café was so popular, she required people to give up their seats after they had been eating fifteen minutes.

"But when—I didn't—" She stopped, hearing her frustrated sputters.

"I should have called everyone," Luke said. "With all the noise and confusion at the end of the meeting, I should have realized some people wouldn't have caught the announcement."

She closed her eyes a moment and then opened them. She could use the excuse that she had been so shocked at being co-chair with him that nothing else had penetrated her mind but she didn't want him to know how much he distracted her.

"Did you have a very large group?"

He hesitated and she knew. "I'm the only one who didn't show up, aren't I?" she asked.

"Tessa, come on, it was an honest mistake."

"Oh, yes." A great way to show people she was responsible and able to coordinate a festival that could draw thousands of people. She couldn't even bother to show up for the first meeting.

He caught her arm just before she entered the hallway. She tried to pull away but his fingers only tightened around her elbow. "Tessa, it's not that big a deal."

She whipped around, her briefcase clipping him on the hip. "Sorry about that," she muttered, frowning at her hands clasping the case. "And I'm sorry I missed the meeting. I'm going to go home, take a long bath, and tomorrow, I'm going to call all the people on the committee and apologize."

"Tessa, you don't have to apologize."

"I do." She glanced at her watch and then studied it again before lifting her head. Her eyes narrowed at him. "That was a very short meeting."

"It's not over. At least, it wasn't when I left."

Her mouth opened and shut several times. "You left the meeting to come find me." She didn't know whether to thank him or wonder about how he knew where she would be.

"Not just you," he said quickly. "I just thought I'd run over here in case anybody got the location mixed up. Bessie was serving snacks while I was gone."

Tessa took a deep breath and let it out slowly. "So I could just ease myself into the meeting without anyone knowing I can't keep track of a single meeting place?"

He rested a light hand on her arm. This time she didn't

shrug him off, finding the action comforting. "It's no big deal," he repeated. "You're a busy woman and you're bound to forget a few things now and then."

He grinned and dragged her toward the hallway, clicking off the light with his free hand. "Come on. If we hurry, we might still get some food."

She discarded several possible explanations during the short drive to Bessie's house at the edge of town. In the end, the simplest seemed best. "Sorry I didn't catch the location," she said with a smile at the small group. "If I don't write something down, it's like I never heard it."

Bessie chuckled and handed her a plate of goodies. "I'm the same way. Reason I could never be a waitress."

"Thank goodness for that," Wilson Pucket said, reaching for another cookie. The dining room table groaned under the delicacies Bessie had prepared and Tessa couldn't believe Luke had been afraid they would all disappear before he returned.

"You can always find a good waitress. Somebody who can cook this good . . ." He made a loud smacking noise and the others laughed.

"Okay?" Luke asked under cover of the laughter. He had taken the chair next to her.

Tessa nodded, her head bent over her plate as if the selection of the right treat to nibble was of paramount importance. The apology had been much easier to make and very easily received. Maybe she was too hard on herself.

"Well, now that we've had some refreshments, let's get back to the meeting," Mabel suggested. She was at least fifteen years older than Tessa, a relative newcomer to the community after her marriage to Fred, a local man. They owned connecting shops that specialized in clothes for men and clothing for women and children. "I promised the kids I'd look at their homework before they went to bed."

Tessa placed her empty plate on the end table next to her and opened her briefcase. "So, what have you decided? Did you come up with any specific activities yet? I don't think we should have much trouble with the Founders Day idea but if you have another one . . ." She glanced over the opened case at the group sitting around her.

Nobody spoke. After a moment, she glanced at Luke. "Luke?"

He gave her a sheepish grin. "Actually, the reason we were waiting for you is that we didn't know what direction to go."

"You haven't done anything?"

"We met everybody," Mabel put in from her place across the room on the sofa. "I didn't realize Coach Hunter owned part of the Sports Shack."

Tessa gave Luke a glance from under her lashes. Coach Hunter. She didn't usually think of him that way.

"Well, if you haven't made any decisions yet . . ." She studied the notes she had written over the past few weeks. "The Founders Day Festival could work," she murmured, "but it would be nice if we could find a more up-to-date focus, too. Too bad we don't know any country singers. We could probably draw in a crowd that way."

"My cousin is Natalie Upman."

Tessa's head jerked up. "What did you say, Mabel?"

"My cousin is Natalie Upman."

"I didn't know that."

"Who is Natalie Upman?" Luke whispered.

Tessa shifted in her chair. "For any of you who don't know," she said, trying not to sound smug, "Natalie Upman is one of the most promising young country singers around."

She smiled at Mabel. "Was it last year when she won the award for best newcomer?"

Mabel nodded, her face wreathed in a proud smile. "She was always singing, everywhere we went. She's actually the daughter of my cousin but we've always been really close. If you're interested, I could see if she would like to sing. Of course, it would depend on the date."

"Mabel, if she can come, we'll work around her schedule," Tessa promised. "Having Natalie Upman here would be a great draw."

"I'll call her tomorrow," Mabel promised. "She was planning to visit anyway. She hasn't seen our kids in a year and she hates being away that long."

The committee broke up soon after that, agreeing that they couldn't do much else until they knew the date and possible appearance of Natalie. Tessa and Luke helped Bessie take the dishes out to the kitchen and then she shooed them away, saying she would rather do her own housekeeping so she knew where everything was.

They walked out together, a tiny remnant of her earlier uneasiness with him hovering around like a pesky gnat. She wanted to be friends with him but her wayward emotions kept skittering in another direction. Tessa kept her briefcase between them, an effective barrier to anything warmer.

"Not a bad meeting," Luke said as they neared her car.

She nodded. "If we can get Natalie, that will show a lot of people this thing will work."

He leaned an arm on the top of her car. "That's important to you, isn't it?"

She paused, her keys dangling from her fingers. Only his profile was visible in the moonlight, his expression hidden in the shadows. "What do you mean?"

"This festival. I wonder if it's more for yourself or for the town."

Her back stiffened. "If we don't do something soon, the downtown will die. Yes, it is partly personal since I've invested a lot in my shop. But that's not the only reason. Or the main one."

"Tessa, lighten up. I'm not saying you're doing anything wrong. Just that you don't have to live and breathe this project. Your shop is doing great; you've started the DBC. You don't have to prove yourself anymore."

"I don't know what you mean." She hoped her words had conveyed the right amount of confusion and dignity.

"Tessa."

His tone reminded her of all the times he had been upset with her or Christine for being in his things, for bothering him, for just being! She leaned over and jammed her key into the lock. "If you don't mind, I'd like to get home."

Her words were clipped and she could barely manage to unlock the door with the hurt twisting through her. *I thought we were on an equal footing. But now he's treating me just like he did when I was a kid.* The words tumbled through her mind and she wished she had the courage to say them out loud.

"Hey, come on, what's the matter?" He caught her arm just above the elbow. "What did I say?"

She wrenched away from him, banging her elbow on the edge of the car door. Tingles shot up her arm and she blinked several times to stop the involuntary tears. She turned her back on him and wrapped her arms around her middle, rubbing the throbbing elbow with her fingers.

"Tessa?"

His hands on her shoulder, his tone gentle, he carefully turned her around. The moonlight played over his features and she could see the concern in his eyes. She considered fighting him but she was just too tired, too frustrated, to follow his mood swings. And her elbow still smarted.

"Whoever said this is your funny bone sure had a warped sense of humor," she managed between clenched teeth.

"Actually, it didn't get the name because it's funny," Luke began in what she was beginning to recognize as his teacher voice.

She shook her head, her irritation draining away as quickly as it had come. He was so . . . reliable. "Luke, I know that. I was trying to ignore the pain."

His fingers slid down her arm and rested on her elbow, his thumb moving in a slow, circular pattern. "Does that help?"

She couldn't stop herself. A giggle spilled over her lips. "It might. But it's the wrong elbow!"

He arched an eyebrow. "Really?" His other hand repeated the same motion, sliding down her arm until his thumb rested in the crook of her elbow. "Here?" he asked softly.

She nodded, her lips trembling at the intent look on his face. His eyes never leaving hers, his hands lightly caressed her arms from the elbows to the wrists and back again, his touch feather-light against her skin.

An owl hooted from behind her and she jumped. "It's okay," he breathed, his mouth moving toward her, his hands slowly drawing her closer. "Just an owl."

"I know that." Her lips were dry and the words came out whisper soft.

A car squealed around the corner and bathed them in its headlights. His head was slanted, his lips only inches away. . . . *This time,* she thought, her eyes starting to close, *this time I'll know what it's like to kiss him.*

"Hey, Coach Hunter! Looking good!"

Luke jumped back as if he had been burned, his hands dropping to his sides. The car spun past, the occupants hanging out of the windows, their loud cries echoing on the still night.

Jolted, she staggered to catch her balance and saw Luke standing a foot away from her. He jammed his hands into his pants pockets. "So, I suppose we should get going. We both have early mornings tomorrow."

She stared at him. His head bent, he scuffed one sneakered foot along the ground. The moonlight glinted on the light streaks of his hair, reflecting the sparks that still floated around them.

The car squealed around another corner, the laughter floating back on the still night. She watched him but he stayed in the same bowed position. *Fine,* she thought, gathering her dignity around her again. *If he wants to pretend nothing just happened, then I can do the same thing.*

She reached down and opened her car door, forcing herself to do it slowly and not with the amount of force she wanted to show. Her parents and friends would be surprised at the show of temper she was feeling.

Are you mad at him or you? an imp in her brain asked. *Didn't you want to stay friends because of Christine? Maybe he's having the same second thoughts. You should probably thank those kids for interrupting you.*

"So, I guess I'll talk to you after you hear from Mabel," he continued, his foot scraping away another layer of dirt from Bessie's yard.

She fought the urge to use her own foot to erase all of his work. Was he glad they had been interrupted? Or was he as frustrated as she was? Had he just been taking advantage of the moment or was he interested in her?

But she couldn't ask any of those things. She didn't want to hear the answers yet. She plastered a smile on her face and climbed into the car. "As soon as I hear from her, I'll let you know," she promised in her sweetest tone.

Her door shut with a decisive click and he jerked in reaction. Her mood lightened. She gave him a jaunty wave, just in case he had lifted his head, and drove off.

"Of all the confusing, frustrating, annoying . . ." She blew out her breath, trying to think of another appropriate adjective.

Once she arrived home, her mind switched to a picture of Luke teasing Anna, helping Bessie with the dishes, listening to Wilson's detailed account of his day. "Ahh!" She shook her head and marched up the stairs, switching off the lights on her way.

She yanked open her dresser drawer and tugged out a pair of pajamas. "It's a good thing that car came by just then. What if we had kissed? Then where would we be?"

She lifted one finger and traced her lips. A soft sigh escaped. "Who am I kidding?" she whispered. "If that car hadn't come by just then, I'd have kissed him without even looking back."

She clutched the pajamas to her chest and stared at her reflection in the dresser mirror. Her eyes were dark and wide, the pupils dilated. Wisps of hair curled around her face, freed from the tight confines of her braid.

"What is he doing to me?" She leaned her hands on the dresser top, the soft flannel material warm under her fingers. What was the matter with her? He was the big brother of her best friend and he could irritate her with a single word. But for several moments, she hadn't been thinking of him as Christine's brother. And the irritation had been of a completely different sort.

Get a grip, she told herself as she pushed off the dresser and went into the bathroom to get ready for bed. Imagine being around Luke every day. Growing up, she had sometimes envied Christine her large family but at the end of a visit, she liked going home to her quiet house where she was the only child. Sharing a house with someone so intimately was a very definite drawback to marriage.

She froze. Marriage! Where had that thought come from? Her heart pounding, she reminded herself it had been one almost-kiss, nothing more.

"It's because of Mandy and Christine," she grumbled, resuming her routine. "They think everybody has to be married just because they are. Well, we can still be friends without me joining their ranks. Just look at how I could help Christine at a moment's notice without any problem. Couldn't do that if I had to answer to a husband or children."

But Luke was there, too, that nagging part of her brain reminded her. And he was a great help.

She scrubbed at her face. She knew talking aloud was a sign of someone going off the deep end but the quiet of the house left her too much time for thinking. She was not about to give Luke anymore of her precious time.

The phone rang just as she was crawling into bed. Punching the ON button, she tucked it under her chin. "Hello."

"Hi, honey."

"Mom!" She settled against the pillows, the blanket tucked around her waist. "It's not Friday; what are you calling for?" She raised off the pillows, her heart speeding up. "Dad's okay, right?"

"He's fine, relax, Tessa." Karen Montgomery's sigh rumbled over the line. "Tessa, honey, you don't have to carry the weight of the world on your shoulders."

First Luke, now her mother. Did she worry about others

too much? Was that possible? "It's just that this is out of the routine," she said.

"I know. I just felt like calling you, see how things are going. Everything okay back there?"

For a moment, Tessa considered telling her mother about the evening. Her mother always seemed to know when she needed to talk. And it would help if she had someone else's opinion about Luke and his behavior. Maybe she was blowing things out of proportion. A good-night kiss didn't mean anything serious nowadays.

She hesitated. What would she say? *I almost kissed Luke? I think he almost kissed me?*

Which would raise a whole lot of questions in her mom's mind. And a lot of hope. Her mother didn't come right out and ask her if she was interested in getting married but Tessa knew each time they attended the wedding of one of her friends, her mother would get all teary-eyed and give Tessa looks that made her uncomfortable.

She opted to talk about the meeting instead. "Did you know Mabel Russell is a cousin of Natalie Upman?"

"The country music singer?"

"The very same. Seems they're pretty close. We're not saying anything yet but Mabel thinks Natalie might come to the festival."

"Oh, Tessa, that would be wonderful!"

Her mother's enthusiasm was balm to her spirit. She relaxed against the headboard and gave her mom news about the town, listening while her mother talked about the places they had seen. They were going to her great-aunt's house for the weekend and then take a load to the Great Lakes region. After that, they would be home for a few days.

"Oh, you'll miss Christine's housewarming party," Tessa said when she heard the dates.

"I know. But your father hated to travel all the way back with an empty load and this way, we can take some time off later and not worry about the money."

Tessa felt a twinge of concern. Her parents had never talked about finances with her and she had assumed they were doing fine. But her mother had quit her job to travel with her husband over the last eight years.

"Mom, the shop is doing really well," she began.

Her mother's laugh echoed over the line. "Tessa, that's sweet but we're not that desperate. In fact, we're not desperate at all. We've just been thinking about doing something different, not so much driving, you know, at least not for work. We're ready to take some time for ourselves."

"If you're sure . . ."

"Actually . . ." Her mother paused and Tessa waited, wondering why she suddenly had a knot in her stomach. "We have been thinking about selling the house."

Tessa stared at the new wallpaper she had just put up. "Selling the house?"

"Not right away. But since you'll probably be getting your own place soon . . ." She paused again and Tessa smiled in spite of herself.

"Subtle, Mom. And here I thought you were turning over a new leaf."

Her mother sighed. "Tessa, dear, you are twenty-six years old. A mother can dream, can't she?"

So can her daughter, Tessa thought, even though she didn't want to dwell on what her dreams might be.

"So, are you seeing anyone?"

Tessa glanced at the clock next to her bed. "I think this must be some sort of a record. Almost fifteen minutes before you asked me."

"Very funny." Her mother waited a beat. "So?"

Again Tessa debated about telling her mother about Luke. Then she remembered a half-hearted promise she had given just the other day. "Well, I'm going with Gary Templar to Christine's housewarming party." They had talked about the party on the way back to her shop after lunch. No need to add that she had agreed to escort him so that he could meet people.

"Really?"

Tessa felt a moment's worth of guilt at the excitement in her mother's voice and then tamped it down. There was no reason her relationship with Gary couldn't develop into something more serious. She enjoyed the times they went out to lunch and she liked his sense of humor.

He was charming and good-looking. Not in Luke's rugged, athletic, open style. Gary was darker, leaner, more mysterious. Once they arrived at Christine's party, she didn't doubt that all the single women would immediately migrate toward them.

Of course, why you're comparing him to Luke, I don't know, she scolded herself silently. *An almost-kiss doesn't mean you have a relationship with Luke. And going out with Gary doesn't make you crazy afterward, talking to yourself, questioning everything that happened.*

She faked a huge yawn that quickly became a real one. "Sorry, Mom, it's been a long day. It's two hours later here, remember?"

"All right." Tessa grinned at the resignation in her mother's voice. "But don't think I've finished with you, young lady."

Tessa laughed. "You do realize that threat hasn't worked on me for, oh, at least fifteen years?"

Her mother's laugh trickled across the miles. "It's always worth a shot. Your father says hello and we love you."

Tears pricked the back of her eyelids. Talking to herself was no substitution for the real thing. "I love you, too, Mom. Tell Dad to drive safe and give Aunt Sylvia my love."

The phone back on the nightstand, she leaned against the pillows and stared at the ceiling. Her parents' plans to sell the house didn't surprise her. She had been more surprised that they had kept it while they were traveling.

What would she do? She didn't think any of the apartments above the stores downtown were available. Even if one was empty, she couldn't imagine living there after the freedom and privacy of the large house.

She clicked off the light and punched her pillow into a ball, turning on her side until she was comfortable. Her mom had said they weren't making any plans right now. No reason to get upset about things or start worrying about where she would live until they did.

Feeling a little like Scarlett, she decided to think about it another day.

Chapter Five

Tessa's grin made it difficult to talk. "It's all right, Mabel. I'm not surprised it took you a few days to catch her. So she can come in August?" she managed, forcing her lips to relax.

"Any time the first two weeks," Mabel confirmed. "She suggested we pick a date right away, though, so she can tell her agent."

A calendar hung on the wall above her office desk and she flipped it forward until it showed August. Only one square was filled, the date of her father's birthday. "Do you think it would be okay if we waited until the next DBC meeting and let everyone help make the decision? We could let her know within the week that way."

"I'm sure that would work," Mabel said.

Tessa thanked her again and hung up the phone, bouncing to her feet and twirling around the room. Fern poked her head in, the beaded curtain draped around her shoulders. "Good news?"

"The best!" Tessa grabbed Fern's hands and twirled her in an impromptu dance. "Natalie Upman can come in August and would love to be part of the first annual Durant Founders Day Festival."

"My, that's a mouthful," Fern said, her words breathless from being twirled around.

Tessa laughed, her feet barely touching the floor as she hummed Natalie's most recent hit, about a love that was true if only he would listen. "Once we have a date, we can start advertising around the area. We'll need a logo, some pictures, a schedule of events—"

"Is this a private party or can anyone join?"

She turned her head and saw Luke standing inside the doorway, long strands of colored beads flowing over his tall, lanky form, the colors reflecting rainbows from the office lights on his dark pants and striped shirt. A few strands filtered through his hair, catching the light and tossing it back in a halo effect.

She bit the inside of her cheek to keep from grinning at that outlandish idea. Anyone less angelic than Luke Hunter, she didn't know.

Not that it mattered today. Today even Luke Hunter was one of her favorite people.

He stepped farther into the room and the beads slipped off his dark blond hair with a whisper, waving gently behind him before they settled back into their concealing curtain. "What's going on?"

"Natalie can come," she sang out.

"Really? When?"

His matter-of-fact tone brought her back to earth. She

released Fern's hands and stepped back to her desk. "Sorry, Fern, I didn't mean to get carried away."

"It was fine." Fern smoothed down her skirt and patted her hair back into place. "I haven't danced like that in ages." She glanced from Tessa to Luke. "I'll just go back to the front," she murmured.

Luke held the curtain open for Fern and scooted out of her way as she hurried into the front of the shop. Tessa sat down in her chair, her earlier jubilation dwindling in the wake of Luke's detached attitude. Now that she was face-to-face with him, she didn't know what to say. Their almost-kiss hung between them, a silent barrier that loomed as heavy and dark as a brick wall.

Their *second* almost-kiss, she realized with a shock.

"So, what do we do now?" he asked as the curtain fell back into place.

Her eyes widened and she half-rose out of her chair. He wanted to talk about what happened that night?

He nodded toward the back wall. "Did you give Mabel a date?"

For a moment, she didn't understand what he was talking about. Glancing over her shoulder, she saw the calendar still turned to August.

She dropped back into her seat and picked up a pencil, rapping it on the edge of the desk. She could be professional, too. "We thought we could wait until the next DBC meeting, since it's only a couple of days away," she said. "Since we need everyone's help, it would probably be best to have the whole committee vote on a date."

He leaned against the wall, his hands tucked into his front pockets. "Might be better to just give them a few choices. Otherwise, we could be there all night while everyone checks their schedules."

She knew he was right. "How do we set the date, then?"

"We could just close our eyes and point." He closed his eyes and waved his finger toward the calendar until it landed on a space.

She rolled her chair backward until she could read the calendar. "Maybe that's not the best way, Luke. You've landed on the name of the month."

He opened his eyes and bent forward, his shoulders inches away from her face, and studied the calendar. "Okay, next idea." He folded one arm over his chest and tapped the page of the calendar with the index finger of his other hand. "A weekend would probably be best, don't you think?" he asked.

She nodded, her voice tight inside, mesmerized by his hand. His aftershave wafted around her and she clenched her hands together in her lap. He was giving no indication that anything had happened between them, and she desperately needed to follow his lead.

"She can come anytime the first two weeks," she said, pleased her voice was only slightly higher than her normal pitch.

"Okay." He leaned closer, his lips pressed together as he stared at the calendar.

Tessa watched him, wondering what he was thinking about so intently. They only needed to consider two weekends. Was he going through his own summer schedule?

She shifted in her chair, her foot accidentally bumping against his. A muscle quivered at his jaw. She lifted her chin. So he wasn't as calm and collected as he wanted her to think. Feeling a tiny bit smug, she let her foot nudge his again before she moved it back under her chair, watching the muscle jump again.

He backed away from her desk and leaned against the

file cabinet, his arms folded over his chest. "Do you have a preference?" he asked.

She shrugged, one corner of her mouth threatening to curve up. Now that she knew his own nonchalance was faked, it was easier to pretend. "Not really. I'm not going anywhere this summer."

One eyebrow arched. She'd never noticed how much darker they were than his hair. "No vacation?"

She shook her head. "I'll take a few days off here and there but summer is my busiest time."

"What about Fern?"

She frowned, not sure what he meant at first, and then her expression relaxed. "She's doing a great job but I wouldn't want to leave her alone for too much time." She leaned forward, her voice lowered. "I trust her completely, but . . ." She lifted her hands, palms up, hoping he would understand.

"It's still your baby."

Her stomach clenched on the word "baby." Was he right? Was she treating her store like it was her child, not letting anyone, even Fern, have a part of it?

She didn't like the image. Her mother might think she had no desire to get married and have a family but Tessa had always dreamed of the same things her friends had wanted. She wanted children, a husband, a life outside her shop.

Which was probably why she was looking at Luke in a different way, she thought in relief. With Abby, Christine, and Mandy all married, with children, and more on the way, she was feeling a little left out. Luke just happened to be around.

She gave him a genuine smile of friendship. "You know, you're right, I have been a little possessive. Maybe by the time summer rolls around, I'll feel comfortable letting Fern watch the place and I'll be able to go off for more than a few days."

Luke blinked. "Did you just agree with me?"

She tipped her head to one side, considering his question. "I guess I did."

He slapped a hand against his forehead. "I think that's twice in one month." He bent forward and peered at her face. "Okay, tell me what you've done with the real Tessa Montgomery."

She pushed at his shoulders. This Luke she could handle. "Very funny. Now, if you didn't have anything else to say to me, good-bye. I have work to do." She shifted her chair until it was facing the desk again.

"Actually, I did have a favor to ask."

She swiveled around. "A favor? Of me?" She pressed her hand against her chest. "Now, this is too much."

"Okay, we're even." He settled into Fern's empty chair, his long legs stretched in front of him, his running shoes almost touching Tessa's pumps.

"Mom and Dad's anniversary is coming up," he continued after a moment's pause. "They're going on a cruise next month."

She nodded. "Christine told me."

"Did she tell you anything else?"

Tessa's brows drew together in concentration, trying to remember what else his sister had said. She seemed to have trouble with her memory lately. "She said they refused a party, that they would rather get away from everything for a few days."

He nodded, drumming the fingers of his right hand on the edge of Fern's desk in a slow rhythmic pattern, his eyes focused on a point behind Tessa.

One corner of her mouth quirked up. She had watched him drum his fingers on the Hunters' dining room table hundreds of times, usually while trying to get out of some trouble that he had landed in or convince his parents that he had a perfectly legitimate request. The speed of his fingers had always seemed to her directly related to the importance of the situation or his appeal.

His fingers were moving at a more-than-average pace right now, which meant whatever he was thinking about mattered to him. So why had he come to her? Except for their forced position as co-chairs, the only thing they had in common was his sister, Christine. . . .

Her heart caught in her throat. Christine and the baby. "Is something the matter with Christine?" she asked in a hurried voice.

He lifted his head and stared at her. "Christine? This isn't about her." He rubbed his chin a moment and then dropped his hand back in his lap. "Actually, it is, in a way."

She pressed her hand against her stomach, taking slow, easy breaths. "Luke, you are making me crazy. Just say it."

He leaned forward, his hands loosely clasped between his knees. "We want to redecorate the living room while Mom and Dad are gone and surprise them. But since Christine hasn't been feeling well—" He lifted both hands in the air. "I don't think she should be doing much. What with working and taking care of Anna already."

"So she's not doing any better?" Since the evening she had watched Anna, she hadn't seen Christine. They had talked on the phone several times but Christine hadn't said anything about her condition.

"A little. She doesn't seem to be as sick. Greg thinks she was off about two weeks on her due date so she's still in the middle of the first trimester. He said she'll probably be over the morning sickness sometime within the next month or so."

Tessa stared at him in surprise. "I do teach health," he muttered, his ears turning red.

She chuckled. "It's okay. I just—" She shook her head. "I just never thought about you knowing about babies."

"And what is that supposed to mean?"

She lifted her hands. "Nothing."

After her earlier thoughts, she definitely didn't want to think about Luke and babies. It would be too easy to picture him with a smiling toddler on his lap, the little child's blond bangs drooping over its forehead, green eyes the exact color of moss in the summer sunlight. . . .

She quickly folded her hands in her lap, forcing her thoughts back to their conversation. "So, how does Christine's health affect me and your redecorating plans?"

"Christine planned to do most of it but like I said, she hasn't been feeling up to much of anything. And if Greg is right, she won't be feeling up to anything until about the time Mom and Dad get back from their cruise."

"You know, decorating their house while they're gone can be tricky," she said carefully. "Don't you think your parents would like to have some say in what happens?"

He straightened up, his embarrassment gone. "They will."

Her eyes widened. "Then how will it be a surprise?"

"That's the great part. Christine has been asking Mom all kinds of questions about decorating while they've been designing her house. She's made list after list of Mom's suggestions."

He reached into the front pocket of his slacks and pulled out a stack of folded notebook paper. Tessa took the pages from his hand and unfolded them to see Christine's neat handwriting.

She scanned the first two pages and then lifted her head to see Luke watching her intently. "This is crazy. There must be a dozen variations listed here."

"That's why we need your help." He leaned forward, his clasped hands dropping between his knees. "When Christine first made the suggestion, I thought we could just use Mom's ideas and do things ourselves. But then she ended up with so many ideas." He shrugged. "Christine thought maybe you could see a pattern, figure out how to use some of the ideas so that we know we're doing what Mom and Dad would like."

For all its good intentions, the plan had to be nipped in the bud. "Luke, it's a nice idea but you could spend a lot of time and money—"

"Tessa," he interrupted, "you know our house. You probably spent more time there than at your own place." She frowned, wondering if he was being critical, but he continued without any notice. "Think about Mom and Dad, what they like. Look at the notes Christine took. If you think it can't be done, we'll take your word for it. But we thought it would be nice to do something for Mom and Dad after all they've done for us."

His voice trailed off and she gave him a suspicious look. If she didn't know him so well, she would think he was completely innocent of any sneakiness, that he was stating a genuine concern for his parents.

But she did know him. From the moment she had walked into his house as a kindergartner, he had gone out of his way to annoy her. Not at first, she corrected herself, remembering those early days. She had been thrilled about going to Christine's house, thinking it would be wonderful to have big brothers. An only child, she could only imagine what it would be like to have other children in the same house.

She had been disappointed the first few times she had visited. Seth had given her some sort of greeting and disappeared with his own friends. Luke had completely ignored her, too grownup at ten to have much to do with two five-year-old girls. And over the next twenty-some years, he had never failed to show her that his opinion hadn't changed, that she was still his kid sister's friend.

"Why did Christine send you?" she asked, breaking off the memories. They would only lead into more recent memories that she didn't want to consider.

His grin spread over his face slowly, ending with a sparkle in his moss-green eyes, the only trait besides his lanky height that he shared with his sister. "Why not?"

"Because she knows how well we get along?"

His bark of laughter echoed in the room. "Precisely."

Her brows snapped together. "What?"

"If Christine came in, you would look over the list and then politely convince her to wait until Mom and Dad were back or maybe try again next year when she wasn't sick. She would agree, since she wouldn't believe her best friend would ignore a request for help, without a good reason, especially when she knows how poorly Christine feels."

Tessa opened her mouth but he continued before she could say anything. "With me . . ." He let the words trail off and lifted his hands, the corners of his eyes crinkling upward.

"With you . . ." She paused, trying to think of an analogy appropriate enough for him. "I'd be completely honest," she finally managed.

"And see it as something of a challenge."

It would be an intriguing project. She loved the cozy feel of the Hunters' house, the lived-in look that had been part of the decor for years. But it would be nice to update the furniture, enliven the color scheme. . . .

She took a deep breath and released it slowly. Being around Luke that much more would be the bigger challenge. And she didn't think she could add that to her life.

"Luke, I want to help, but without your mom . . ." She lifted her hands, palms up. "And with running the shop, planning the festival—"

"Just look at the list," he broke in. "Think about it before you make a decision."

He stood up and she quickly straightened from the desk. She had to look up to meet his eyes. "Luke, I can tell you right now—" she started.

He leaned over and tapped her on her nose. Her breathing stuttered and she backed up to get away from him. She bumped into the hard edge of the desk, halting her retreat.

"I'll talk to you in a few days," he said quietly. "Please don't decide yet."

The curtain rattled as he walked through it. She stared at the rustling beads and then glanced back at the list. "You're not going to con me into this," she muttered. "No matter how sweet you are. I am not going to help redecorate your mother's living room without her there."

"Did you say something, dear?"

Tessa lifted her head and met the clear gaze of her assistant. "Just thinking aloud," she said.

Fern nodded. "I find that helps me work out problems, too." She pushed the chair Luke had moved back into place and sat down. "What did Coach Hunter want?"

Tessa silently thanked Fern for using Luke's title. It gave

her the distance she needed to look at the problem less personally. "He just stopped by to give me a message from his sister."

"That was nice of him." Fern glanced over her shoulder. "The students think the world of him. And he's very good-looking, isn't he?"

Tessa shrugged. "I guess so."

"You've known him for a long time, haven't you?"

Tessa knew where this conversation was going. Did Fern and her mother talk to each other? "Which is why I would never be interested in dating him, Fern." Even if they had almost shared a couple of kisses that haunted her sleep at night.

She grinned when Fern's mouth dropped open in a delicate O. "I know you think he's perfect but to me, he'll always be Christine's big brother. And he thinks of me as her pesky little friend."

"But now that you're both adults—" Fern began, but Tessa raised a hand and the words stopped.

"Nothing's changed. Luke doesn't see me as a romantic interest any more than I do." She pushed away the memory of standing by her car, the moonlight beaming down around both of them, his lips hovering above hers. An accident of the night, nothing else, she told herself.

"Besides," she added, "I don't have time, not with all the work the shop needs. And he still calls me munchkin, for goodness' sake." Even though the hated nickname hadn't sounded so annoying the last time he'd used it.

"Probably so you don't see how he really feels."

Tessa laughed. "A nice thought, Fern, but Luke has never been one to hide his feelings. You've heard the way we bicker whenever we're next to each other. We're not inter-

ested in each other that way. Which is fine with me," she
added quickly, when she saw Fern's mouth open.

She shifted in her chair until she was facing the desk.
"Now I'm going to see if I can reconcile this bank statement. If you could mind the shop for a little bit, we can
then go over the orders you've been making."

Effectively canceling any more discussion about her personal life, she picked up her pencil and determinedly studied the figures on the list in front of her.

By the time the phone rang that evening, she was ready
for Christine. "Hi. I thought I had a few days."

"What are you talking about? I just called to see how
things were going."

She grinned at her friend's innocent tone. "Won't work,
Christine."

Christine laughed. "Okay, so you know why I'm calling.
Luke said you weren't very helpful."

"That's not true! He tried to use guilt, you know."

"He learned from one of the best."

Tessa chuckled and sank down on the kitchen chair.
"Should I tell your mom you said that?"

"No!"

"Okay, your secret's safe with me." She kicked off her
shoes. She really needed to invest in some comfortable
pairs. Maybe Luke was the smart one, with his running
shoes. She was the boss, she could make her own dress
code.

She knew Christine was waiting for her to say something. "I told Luke the idea was good but your mom should
be actively involved," she offered.

"Did you look at my notes?" Christine demanded.

Tessa chewed on her lower lip, wishing she had thought

to bring the list home with her. "Yes." She wasn't exactly lying. She had glanced at them when Luke first gave her the list.

"Then you can see I have enough information to decorate Mom's entire house. Which I would do, if I thought we had enough time."

"But Christine, if you were talking to her while making decisions about your place, that doesn't mean the details would work at her house."

"I knew you didn't look at the list," Christine sputtered. "I specifically asked her what she would do if she could redo *her* house."

"You did?"

"I did." Tessa could imagine Christine nodding her head in emphasis, her red curls bouncing around her face. "At first, I just wanted to avoid some of the problems they had and then I realized we could give them a great anniversary present."

"But giving possibilities isn't the same as actually making decisions," Tessa said, knowing her argument would carry no weight with Christine.

She wished she had looked at the list more before she had to deal with Christine. But the bank statement had taken her longer than she had expected and then she and Fern had found it difficult to pare down the order she had made. By then, she had just wanted to get home, slip off her shoes, and relax.

"Luke said I had a few days to decide," she said in her defense.

Which was probably part of their strategy. They probably thought they could just work on her like a dripping faucet until she finally decided to get up and do something about it. "I don't think you should redecorate their house when

they're not home," she added stubbornly when Christine
didn't say anything.

"Then why are you doing your mom's place?"

She plopped against the back of the chair, the legs wob-
bling, and stared at the wallpaper books and paint chips
stacked against one wall of the kitchen. Her redecorating
wasn't the same thing at all. Her parents didn't care about
the house, especially if they were considering selling it. But
she couldn't tell Christine that yet.

"Because," she managed.

Christine laughed. "What are you, six? 'Because' won't
work anymore. Come on, Tessa, this will be fun. And Luke
and I will take all the blame if Mom and Dad hate it. Not
that they will. Mom thinks you're absolutely wonderful
when it comes to decorating ideas."

"Flattery will get you absolutely nowhere," Tessa stated,
but the statement lacked heat. A tiny spurt of anticipation
was growing in her and she knew it was only a matter of
time before she gave in.

"Mom and Dad don't leave for a month," Christine said,
"and then they'll be gone for ten days. That should give us
plenty of time to get things organized and Luke said he
could get some friends to help move furniture, paint, that
kind of thing."

"Oh, I can just imagine the help they'll give."

"Tessa, come on, you know you're going to do this. Why
prolong our agony?"

Tessa closed her eyes and sighed deeply. Opening them,
she stared at her fingers drumming on the table.

Her fingers were definitely moving up and down in a
steady pattern. She couldn't remember ever drumming her
fingers before.

Oh, this is great, she thought. *Now I'm picking up his*

bad habits. He'll drive me crazy before we're done. He'll hang around, make silly suggestions, try to be funny. . . .

Her breath whooshed out in another long sigh. And if he didn't do that, she ran a risk of a repeat of their almost kisses. She didn't know which one bothered her the most anymore. "Christine, you know I can't work with Luke. I'm already strained to the limit with the Festival Committee."

Silence. Tessa wondered if she had hurt her friend's feelings. Christine just didn't seem to understand how much Luke bothered her. She probably should have outgrown it by now but since she hadn't, Christine would just have to face facts. Chemistry or not, she couldn't be together with Luke in the same room for very long without disagreeing about something.

"Not even for Mom and Dad?" Christine asked quietly. "And me?"

Tessa didn't answer right away. She padded over to the counter and filled a glass of water from the tap, drinking it and putting the glass into the sink before speaking. "That is not even fair."

Christine's chuckle sounded over the line and Tessa wished she had been able to keep her mouth shut. She had no way of backing down now.

"I'll come over tomorrow evening," Christine said. "You can tell me which ideas you think would work best together."

Tessa tried one more time. "Christine—"

"Gotta go, Jake's home. 'Bye."

The phone went dead. Tessa stared at it until the recorded voice reminded her to hang up and try again.

Clicking the phone off, she plodded across the kitchen floor in her stocking feet and hung it up. "You do not have to do this," she reminded herself, even though she knew she was already committed. "You can pick and choose your projects."

She wandered into the living room, stepping over the stool she had left near the door. The furniture was pushed into the middle of the room so that she could paint the walls and she had to climb over the hassock to reach the couch. She stretched out, her head on one armrest and her feet on the other, and stared at the ceiling.

It could be fun, she thought, her mind drifting into the positive. The Hunters' living room was large and spacious, with windows across one side that overlooked the front yard. The furniture was comfortable but it was showing signs of age and she didn't think they had bought a new couch in all the time she had been going to their house. She wouldn't have to do anything drastic, just refurbish it a little. Then, if Catherine or Paul didn't like something, it would be a simple matter to change it.

Seth wouldn't give her any problems. He was due home any day but he tended to coast through life, accepting whatever happened. If what Luke said was true, Christine would be happy to have someone else take on the responsibility.

"Besides, she trusts me," Tessa said to the ceiling.

Luke. She couldn't imagine Luke ignoring an opportunity to tease her, but how involved would he be with a decorating project? He might be part of the advance guard but surely his involvement would end as soon as she accepted the job.

Her mind whirling with possibilities, she went back into the kitchen and picked up an empty pad of paper.

* * *

She was not completely surprised to see Luke standing behind Christine when she opened the door, especially after Christine whispered, "He's paying for most of it. I couldn't tell him he couldn't come over."

But she was not about to give him equal say. They might have to work as co-chairs on the Festival Committee but he had come to her for the decorating. "I'll listen to your ideas but Christine has final say. Otherwise, I don't do it."

"You don't think my taste is good enough?" he countered.

Tessa bit her lip but she couldn't stop the snort of laughter. Christine's laugh was more forthright. "Luke, we all know what your apartment looks like," she said.

"I haven't decided on my style yet," he said with his nose in the air.

This time, Tessa's laughter escaped and echoed around the room. "Style? Luke, you paper your wall with sports articles and think running shoes are ornaments."

He cocked his head to one side. "And that's a bad thing?"

She tossed a small pillow at him. He caught it easily with one hand and tucked it behind his head. "Now you, of course, have perfect taste." He waved a hand around the living room. "I really like the addition of the stepstool to that corner and the way you've bunched all the furniture in the middle of the room . . ." He kissed the tips of his fingers with a flourish. *"C'est magnifique!"*

"Ignore him," Christine said, turning away from him. "I don't know why I brought him."

"I have the checkbook," he reminded her, waving it in the air.

Tessa leaned toward Christine. "Do you think you could

make him a silent partner?" she asked in a loud stage whisper.

Christine glanced over her shoulder. "Silent?" She shook her head with a mournful look. "What do you think?"

Tessa eyed him carefully. He sat in the middle of the couch, his arms spread along the back, his feet casually propped on the hassock. His hair was brushed back from his forehead and he was watching them both with a calculating look in his eyes.

A tiny trickle of perspiration started at the base of her neck and slid down her back. One corner of his mouth tipped up in a lopsided grin and she clenched her hands together in her lap.

She couldn't imagine him staying silent a moment longer than necessary. He would be just as much in the way as she had anticipated when she first considered even taking the project.

For some reason she couldn't yet fathom, he was acting like he would stick with the project from beginning to end. Not that he tended to shirk his responsibilities. For all his lighthearted ways, he was one of the most hardworking people she had ever met. But she didn't have any idea why he would want to work on something so different from all his other activities.

Fern's words came back to her and she slanted him a look from under her lashes. Luke didn't have any hidden agenda. He was open and aboveboard. If he was interested in her, surely he would say something, give her a sign. He was just interested in keeping track of his money, she told herself. And for all the teasing that went on between the Hunter children and their parents, she knew they loved one another very much.

He hadn't moved. She glanced away and swallowed.

Luke doesn't have any hidden agenda, she repeated silently. *Especially not one that includes me.*

She didn't want to think about why that thought didn't make her feel better.

Chapter Six

She didn't have any time to think about the decorating tips before the next DBC meeting. First thing in the office Wednesday morning, she did gather up Christine's notes but she only gave them a cursory glance before stuffing them into her briefcase. Fern had called in saying she had a bad case of the flu and Tessa had told her to stay in bed for as long as she needed, not to worry about the shop.

As if knowing she was alone, customers streamed in all morning, some staying long enough to make a purchase, others just browsing around the shop with no particular intent. She smiled and chatted with each one, determined to show them all the same amount of attention. A few people wandered in to ask about Fern and Tessa was amazed again at how quickly news spread in the small town.

Just before noon, the bell over the door jangled as she was writing out a receipt. She lifted her head and met the dark gaze of Gary Templar.

93

"Hi, I'll be with you in a few minutes," she said.

"No problem." He bent over a small display of glass globes she had recently found at an estate auction, picking one up and shaking it so the shimmery crystals floated around.

She completed the sale and thanked the woman for her purchase. After seeing her out the front door, she joined Gary at the display. "I have several others in the back room," she offered. "Do you want to see if they work, too?"

He smiled, placing the globe he was holding back on the baker's rack she used for displaying smaller items. The white, silver, and blue sparkles he had released in each of the globes caught the sunlight coming in the window of the door.

"That's okay. I just wanted to see if I could get them all to snow at the same time." He loosely clasped his hands together behind his back. "I wondered if you were free for lunch."

"Now?"

He glanced around the empty shop. "Seems quiet right now. I have a few phone calls coming in after one o'clock so now works best for me. But if you're busy . . ."

She shook her head. "I've been busy. A break sounds great right now. Fern's out with the flu," she explained, following him out the door, "and I had at least a dozen people come in to ask about her. And if she hadn't called earlier to say she was feeling better, I'd be feeling guilty. At least half of those people ended up buying something!"

"I'm not surprised."

She slanted him a look, her key hovering over the keyhole. "Should I give you a few more minutes to browse?" she asked with a sly grin.

"Not unless you want to pay for your own lunch."

She slipped the key into the door and locked the door. "You drive a hard bargain, counselor." She turned the hands on the small clock in her window to 1:00. "Where are we going?"

"Bessie's Café okay?" he asked.

"Sounds fine to me."

They walked down the street in companionable silence, their strides evenly matched. She felt comfortable with him and she contrasted their easy relationship with the fireworks that usually resulted when she was with Luke.

Not that she wanted to compare the two men. No doubt if she had an older brother, she would react around him just the way she did around Luke. Christine had often moaned and groaned about her older brothers, even going so far as to state that she would be much happier if she had been an only child. Her friends had never believed her even though Tessa had often felt she understood what she meant. Having someone around all the time who knew your history, had stored-up memories of when you weren't at your best . . .

"Sorry I haven't been around for a while." Gary's voice broke into her thoughts.

She gave him a startled look. "That's okay," she said carefully. They had gone out a few times and she liked being with him but she didn't think she had ever given him reason to believe he had to account for his time with her.

"I had to go back to St. Louis for a few days last week and then Kansas City over the weekend."

"I've been pretty busy, too."

They arrived at Bessie's Café. The crowd waiting for tables spilled out onto the sidewalk and he stopped her with a gentle hand on her arm. "What do you think?"

She tipped her head and calculated the number of people

waiting in front of her. "At the most, a thirty-minute wait," she mused quietly.

"I'm game if you are."

Tessa nodded and he moved toward the front of the line, giving his name to the hostess. She wrote it down and then called out the name of the next group.

"So, what have you been doing over the last week?" He motioned to the bench that had just been vacated and she sat down, moving over so he could join her.

"Working. Fern took off a day last week and now she's home with the flu this week. Not that I'm complaining," she added quickly. "It's kind of nice to have the place to myself for a while."

He grinned. "That pride of ownership creeping in again."

Her brows drew together. First Luke and now Gary commenting about how possessive she was of the shop. Was she that wrapped up in the business?

He frowned. "What's the matter?"

"Nothing. I just . . ." She didn't know what to say. He hadn't exactly criticized her. And everyone knew it took a lot of work to make a business successful. "Anyway, what about you? St. Louis and Kansas City in one week? That's a lot of driving."

He gave her a distracted nod, his lips pressed together. "Not what I would call fun," he said cryptically. "At least the weather was good."

She wanted to point out that it was May, not the middle of winter, but he seemed reluctant to discuss his trips.

And you don't need to pry, she told herself. *You hate it when people keep asking you questions. Leave it alone.*

Determined to move the conversation away from more personal topics, she mentioned a ball game she had watched over the weekend, asking if he had any loyalties. They enjoyed a spirited discussion about the chances of the various teams, still arguing goodnaturedly when his name was called.

His hand at the back of her waist, he carefully guided her through the tables in the small café. Most of the patrons were other businesspeople and several greeted both her and Gary before turning their attention back to their food. The chatter vied for attention with the rattling of silverware and the constant shouts of "Order up!"

Gary held her chair for her and waited until she was seated before taking his own place across from her.

"When I was little, I used to play waitress at home," Tessa said in a loud voice over the roar of the others. "I'd carry in the main course and yell 'Order up!' My mom and dad were relieved when I finally passed through that phase."

Gary grinned. "If you bussed your own tables, I would think they'd be thrilled."

She pondered his statement a moment and then shook her head. "I don't think I played that part. Mostly, I think I just liked shouting in the dining room."

His chuckle filtered through the noise. "When did you start playing storekeeper?"

The waitress arrived at their table, forestalling her immediate answer. Bessie operated on the "one entree per day" plan, the only choice offered being that of drink. They gave their orders to her and she promised to be right back with their food.

Tessa leaned forward, her hands folded in her lap. "I don't know if I did play storekeeper," she said, referring back to his question. "I wasn't really interested in business until high school."

"Really?" He leaned back in his chair, one arm casually draped over the back.

"Did you always want to be a lawyer?" she countered.

He stared at the ceiling a moment and then nodded slowly. "I can't remember any other option."

She thought that was a strange way to answer the question, as if the choice had been made by someone other than himself. Before she could ask him any more, the waitress returned, dropping two plates loaded with meatloaf, mashed potatoes, and green beans in front of them.

"Your time starts now," she said with a grin, depositing their drinks on the table.

Tessa glanced at the clock on the wall. "Okay."

"I always feel like I've just entered a race," Gary confessed, his fork halfway to his mouth with a bite of meatloaf.

"You have." Tessa grinned and scooped up a bite of potatoes. "And if you want dessert, I suggest you not talk too much right now."

They had five minutes to spare when they finished the last bites of their main meal. Without missing a beat, the waitress collected their dirty dishes and replaced them with two pieces of apple pie. By the time Tessa had swallowed the last flaky crumb, the busboy was standing behind her chair, his rag already in his hand.

"Somebody should tell Bessie that it takes at least twenty minutes for food to get to your stomach and let your brain know you aren't hungry," she mumbled, licking her fork clean in a moment of defiance before standing up and following Gary toward the front of the café.

"She probably adds in the minutes you wait at the cash register," Gary replied.

"Tessa!"

She turned at the sound of her name. Luke sat at a front table, amid several other high school teachers. "Hi, Luke," she said. No matter what he said to her, she was not going to react.

"I'll meet you at the front door," Gary said, moving forward and getting in line with the others waiting to pay.

"I'll be right there." She shifted back to Luke. If she raced off without saying something else to him, he would think she didn't want to be around him.

Which wasn't exactly true, she thought in surprise. Sparks might fly when they were together but she didn't have to watch her step with him like she did with Gary. Not that their lunchtime conversation hadn't been entertaining but she had felt uncomfortable several times when she had wandered into territory he definitely didn't want to discuss. At least with Luke, she didn't have to watch what she said. He had never backed down from a confrontation with her.

Aware of the curious glances from the others at the table, she smiled. "What are you doing here? School's not out yet, is it?"

He nodded. "Ended this morning. Students went home just before lunch." He spread his hands over the food on their table. "So we decided to go out."

She nodded toward the clock. "You should have gone somewhere else if you wanted a relaxing lunch." Mandy often moaned about how quickly she had to finish her lunch so she could get back to the classroom or outside for recess duty.

"Time is not an issue today," Luke said with a grin. "We're outside the four walls of the school."

Since she knew he loved teaching and would spend part of his summer break teaching classes and tutoring, she just shook her head at him. Glancing over her shoulder, she saw Gary standing by the front door, his hands in his pockets. He smiled at her and with a quick good-bye to Luke and the others, she hurried over to join him.

"That was Coach Hunter, right?" Gary asked as they walked out of the café.

"His sister Christine is one of my best friends," she hastened to explain. Not that she owed him an explanation. But talking to another man while he paid for her lunch seemed rude.

"Christine?" he asked.

"She's having the housewarming this weekend," she said, knowing he was still trying to place all the people that he was meeting. "If you can still go."

They stopped for the red light. "I have it on my calendar," he said. "I may have to meet you there because of a work conflict, though."

She wondered what kind of work he needed to do over Memorial Day weekend but she'd already decided she wasn't going to pry into his private life. "That's okay. I can go early then and help Christine set up."

The light changed and she stepped off the curb. The heel of her shoe caught in a tiny crack and she stumbled. Gary caught her elbow and she wobbled precariously until she had her balance.

"You okay?" he asked, his face only inches away from hers.

Her heart thumped in her chest, her breathing ragged, whether from the near fall or his proximity, she didn't know. "I'm fine, thank you."

She took a step and almost fell again. "What in the world?" She twisted her head and looked down at her shoe, groaning when she saw the broken heel lying on the sidewalk.

Gary followed her glance. Still holding her arm, he bent down and picked up the narrow piece of leather.

"Sole Repair is just across the street," he suggested.

Gently disengaging herself from his hold, she slipped off both shoes and gathered them into one hand. "I really should invest in a pair of tennis shoes," she muttered.

Gary chuckled. "Come on." He motioned toward the street with a wave of his hand. "I'll keep an eye out for any dangerous items."

She picked her way carefully over the hot asphalt. Tiny pebbles imbedded in the tar ripped at the bottom of her stockings. "Christine says walking barefoot causes a lot of the accidents they see in the emergency room during the summer," she said, stepping around several pieces of broken glass he pointed to.

"In your case, shoes seem to be the culprit."

She chuckled, keeping her eyes on the ground. The afternoon sun beat down on her back and she could feel the heat through the thin cotton of her dress. If it was this warm in May, what would June be like? she thought as she hopped onto the curb and inched toward the shoe repair store.

The sidewalk was slightly cooler under her feet. Gary pushed open the door of Sole Repair and she breathed a sigh of relief when her toes felt the cool linoleum floor. "I used to run around barefoot all summer," she said to Gary as he followed her in. "I must be getting wimpy. That walk just about did me in."

"Your feet had a chance to toughen up when you were littler." He reached forward and dinged the small bell sitting on the counter.

Wilson poked his head through the doorway behind the counter, his glasses perched on top of his head and a sandwich in his hand. "Tessa." He disappeared for a moment and returned, the glasses on his nose and the sandwich gone.

"Afternoon." He smiled at her and then frowned at Gary. "Templar, isn't it? The new lawyer?"

Gary nodded. "She lost the heel of her shoe after lunch," he said, putting the offending item on the counter between them.

Tessa added her shoes. "Do you think you can fix it?"

Wilson picked up the broken shoe and the heel, bringing them close together. "Shouldn't be a problem. Won't be ready this afternoon, though."

"That's okay. I think I have an extra pair of shoes in my office." She put her initials on the work form Wilson passed to her.

"You want to borrow a pair of shoes to get back to work?" Wilson asked.

She nodded in relief. "That would be great. I don't think I could make it to the next block barefoot again."

Wilson slipped into the back room and returned with a pair of old-fashioned black galoshes. Half the buckles were missing.

Tessa's lips parted in surprise. She opened her mouth and then snapped it shut. Beggars couldn't be choosers.

"Hope you don't mind my old boots," Wilson said, handing them over the counter to her. "Couldn't find anything else to loan you."

She put the boots on the floor and slid her feet into them. She could easily fit both feet into one boot. "They're fine, Wilson. At least I won't burn my feet. Thanks."

The boots slapped against the floor as she walked. She

didn't look at Gary. She felt foolish enough without seeing the same emotion in his eyes.

"They say black goes with everything," he murmured as they waited for the light to change.

She slanted a glance at him from under her lashes. One corner of his mouth was curled up. He didn't seem to be laughing at her so much as laughing at the situation. "As long as I'm making a fashion statement," she said just as softly.

"I hate to tell you but you are," he said quietly, nudging her arm.

She lifted her head and saw Mr. Owens standing on the sidewalk outside his shop, staring at her strange footwear. *Don't take yourself so seriously*, she thought, drawing on Luke's words. *If Gary can chuckle about this, so can you.*

Straightening her shoulders, she lifted her head and favored him with a bright smile. "Good afternoon. Lovely weather, isn't it?"

Head high, she sailed past, praying one of her boat-sized boots didn't fly off her foot and hit him in the stomach.

Outside her shop, she rummaged in her purse for her key. "Thanks for lunch, Gary. It was fun."

He leaned his shoulder against the outside wall of her shop. "I need to thank you. You provided the entertainment."

She located the key and unlocked the door, pushing it open and switching on the lights. "You really need to get out more," she chided him. "Watching a woman maneuver down the street in a floppy pair of black galoshes should not be the highlight of your day."

He laughed and flicked the tip of her nose with his finger. "I don't know what's going to top it."

His watch beeped and he straightened away from the

wall. "I need to get back. I set my watch so I wouldn't miss those calls." He hesitated and then leaned forward, brushing her lips with a soft kiss. "I'll call you later."

Bemused, she walked into her office, her fingers lightly touching her lips. His kiss had been gentle, tender, almost a question.

Unbidden, the image of Luke sprang to her mind. His lips only inches away from hers. His green eyes crinkling with mischief. Electricity arcing between them.

She groaned and stomped into the back room, kicking off each boot and listening to them land on the floor with a satisfying thud. Why was she thinking of Luke? She might have more history with him but that wasn't necessarily a good thing. Did she want to be with a man who could always dredge up a memory of when she was a bratty little kid pestering him? Better to be with someone who knew her only as an adult, didn't have any preconceptions to ignore.

She dug through the little closet in the back corner and emerged with a worn-out pair of loafers she wore whenever she poked around in the storeroom.

She laced them on and went back into the main room. After the busy morning, the quiet mocked her and she turned up the radio so she didn't have to listen to herself think.

"Fern, you didn't have to come in today," Tessa said the next afternoon.

The older woman unwrapped the scarf she had tied around her hair and looped it over the coat stand in the office. "I knew you wanted some time to get ready for the meeting tonight."

"Fern, I don't need any time." She handed the scarf back

to Fern. "Go home and rest. You're still too pale and I'll feel terrible if anything happens to you."

Fern sniffled and Tessa watched her swallow a cough. "I'm fine, Tessa, really. You can work back here on your notes and I'll just watch the front for you."

"You are going home." Tessa gently turned her around and with her hands still on Fern's shoulders, marched her toward the front door.

"Tessa," Fern pleaded, her face crumbling with the word. "I'm so bored."

Tessa almost relented and then she shook her head. "No, Fern. My mother always said boredom is a state of mind and a reasonably intelligent person could overcome it. You're more than reasonably intelligent or I wouldn't have hired you."

Fern's lips parted and she blinked several times. "Why, that is the sweetest thing I've ever heard."

Tessa grinned and opened the door. "Thank you. Now, please, go home, put your feet up, and come back tomorrow when you're rested."

"You're sure?" Fern's glance darted back to the shop.

"I am. We had a busy morning yesterday but today has been relatively quiet."

"All right. But call me, please, if you need me."

Tessa squeezed her shoulder. "I promise."

She waited until Fern drove off and then shut the door, walking back to the counter, her brow furrowed in thought.

Fern had never mentioned being bored before and Tessa wondered if it had all been a ruse to get her own way or if she really meant it.

Living alone could get boring. She was busy with her shop during the day and the redecorating was taking much of her evenings but there were still lots of moments to fill.

Not that she was bored too often. Her parents had always encouraged her to rely on herself and she found it difficult to give up a lifetime of training.

Which is probably why I won't let Fern do more, she thought with a flash of insight. *I feel like I have to do it all.*

Some of that, she knew, stemmed from her upbringing. She had never felt unloved but her parents formed a connected unit and she was the third wheel. They didn't deliberately exclude her but they had secrets with each other and while she knew that was the way it should be, she could remember times when she felt left out.

Not over big things, she thought, opening a buffet drawer wider and draping a lace doily over the edge. She twitched the cloth a fraction and stepped back to survey the result. More when she saw them exchange a quick smile over something someone had said. Like they had a secret language only they understood.

She moved toward a display of picture frames. Shared memories. Her parents had been together so long, her mother had once said she couldn't even remember what life was like before she met Tessa's dad.

Two of the picture frames had been knocked over while people were browsing and she righted them, moving them around until she felt they had the right symmetry.

Maybe she should let Fern take over the window arrangements. She could help move any furniture but Fern could make the decisions about what was displayed. Fern had invited her for dinner several times since they had started working together and Tessa had been impressed with the organization of Fern's small, neat house. She would tell her when she returned.

She left the shop a little before 5:00. Only a handful of

customers had trickled in during the afternoon and she felt no qualms about closing up shop early.

The lights were already on in the conference room when she arrived for the meeting. Several clusters of people stood around the table and a few greeted her as she moved into the room.

She did a quick sweep of the room but Luke wasn't there. Breathing a little easier, she dropped her briefcase on a chair near the middle of one side of the table and joined a group visiting near the windows.

She knew the moment he walked into the room. She didn't know how she knew or why but the atmosphere changed, she turned, and he was standing in the doorway.

He nodded toward her and she gave him a slight nod in response. Turning back to the group, she smiled and listened, trying to catch the gist of their conversation, all the time aware of Luke just behind her.

She glanced at her watch, wondering when Helen would call the meeting to order. Her mind wandered away from the talk about the coming high school graduation. Most of the committee members had children or grandchildren graduating, and while Tessa knew a few of the students graduating, she didn't have the same degree of interest in the topic.

"Say, Luke," Martin called. "Maybe you can answer our question."

She jolted at the sound of his name and realized he was joining their group. She couldn't walk away now without arousing suspicion, at least on his part.

He paused next to Martin, directly across from her. "What can I do for you?"

"Are they going to have graduation outside this year?"

Luke nodded. "That's the plan. The forecast looks pretty

clear for the next few days. Only a few isolated reports of people predicting rain."

His eyes met Tessa's and he winked.

Why was he looking at her like that? She didn't care if it rained or not. Not that she wanted it to rain for graduation. The ceremony was more enjoyable in the football stadium under a clear evening sky than crammed into the smaller high school gymnasium.

He winked again and her eyes widened. Was he referring to the galoshes she had worn? She gritted her teeth and then telegraphed a message to him. If he had any ounce of consideration for her, he would keep quiet. It was one thing to laugh about the situation with Gary. But to have it come up before she made her presentation . . .

He dipped his chin toward his chest and she breathed a little easier. He wouldn't say anything to the rest of them. And if he did, well, she would just have to tough it out and laugh the loudest.

She didn't know where that thought had come from. She glanced at Luke but he was talking to Wilson now and had his back to her. Were they able to communicate across a crowded room? She had often wondered how her mother and father had known certain things without any words passing between them and she often suspected the same thing happened with her married friends but she had never experienced it before.

Helen asked them to take their seats and she crossed the room to the table, bemused. She moved her briefcase to the floor and then looked up in dismay when she saw Luke sliding into the chair next to her.

"Why do you always do that?" she whispered. Her heart hammered under her blouse and she told herself it was only because she was nervous he would tease her in front of the group. That was a fluke, probably didn't even come from him, she reminded herself. She was dreaming things.

He sat down. "What?"

"Sit by me."

He glanced around the table. Unlike the other meetings, most of the chairs were full. "I thought we should sit together so we can give the report together."

She couldn't think of anything to say to his logic. Dropping her briefcase with a small thud, she sat down and folded her hands on top of the table, staring straight ahead.

"I won't tell anyone," he murmured into her ear.

Her fingers clenched together. All thoughts of laughing the loudest had disappeared. "I can't believe Wilson told you," she muttered as copies of the minutes of the last meeting were passed around the table.

"He didn't."

She shifted until she faced him. "How did you find out then?"

"Arthur."

She leaned forward and looked at the older man sitting at the far end of the table. "Mr. Owens told you?"

Luke nodded. "He said you looked like a little girl dressed up in your daddy's shoes."

"Great." She dropped her gaze to her hands and wished she had a way to gracefully leave the meeting.

"Hey, it's not that big a deal."

"That's because people think you've grown up," she blurted out.

"What are you talking about?"

She lifted her head and favored him with a long look. His eyes watched her carefully, without a hint of his usual humor in them.

"Munchkin," she said slowly.

"Munchkin?" He frowned, his face a mask of confusion. "Don't tell me you don't understand."

He shook his head. "I don't. What does munchkin have to do with galoshes?"

She leaned toward him. The conversation still buzzed around them. "They both remind me that people don't see me as a grownup."

His brow cleared and he leaned back in his chair. "That's not true, Tessa. At least it isn't on my part."

Her eyes narrowed. "You don't call me munchkin because you see me as a little kid?"

"Well, to be honest . . ." His voice trailed off and he grinned. "Okay, you're right. Usually it's just habit. But sometimes . . ."

She started to turn away from him but he caught her elbow. "I still don't understand how this relates to the galoshes."

She nodded toward the other end of the table. "Mr. Owens treats me like I'm one of the kids coming in for treats after school. He came in the other day, trying to convince me that we shouldn't have the festival this year."

Luke shrugged. "That's just his opinion. It has nothing to do with whether you're grown up or not."

"But don't you see? If he's telling everybody about the galoshes, they'll just laugh at anything I suggest. Instead of thinking about my ideas, they'll be seeing me schlepping down the street in too-big shoes."

His eyes twinkled and she could see he was trying to hold back his grin. She lifted her hands in defeat, even though the corners of her mouth were lifting in response. "See?"

"Tessa, come on." He dropped his hand on her clenched

ones. "You just have to laugh at yourself before they have a chance to laugh at you. Then it will just pass away."

A tingle slid up her arms at the echo of the words she had thought earlier. His hand was warm, the skin slightly rough against hers. She froze, unable to breathe or concentrate on anything other than his hand touching hers, his thumb lightly stroking over her knuckles.

She gave herself a mental shake. Luke was just trying to relax her, just like he would Christine. Nothing else. Probably Christine could communicate with him that way, too. Some sort of family connection. And she had spent a lot of time with his family over the years.

She carefully slipped her hands out from under his. "Is that what you do?" she asked, her equilibrium restored.

He gave a slight shrug, barely moving his shoulders, his hand resting on the table between them. "Sometimes. Sometimes I just ignore them." He leaned closer, his breath dancing across her cheek. "Arthur is somebody you could ignore."

Her chin tilted up, considering his remarks. And then something else registered. Luke always called him Arthur.

Luke had shopped at Mr. Owens' store as a child just like she had. He had made the transition to adult by simply using the man's first name.

"You're right." She took a deep breath and let it go quickly. "Excuse me, Wilson?" she said in a slightly louder tone.

The older man paused in his conversation and glanced at her. "Yes?"

"Thank you for the loan of your boots. I'll bring them back tomorrow when I pick up my shoes." She smiled around the table. "Unless Luke here is wrong and we do get rain. Then I may keep them for a while, if you don't mind."

Wilson chuckled and several others joined in. She settled back in her seat, a smile still on her face.

"Not bad."

Her eyebrows lifted in surprise, both at herself and his compliment. "It wasn't, was it? Thanks for the tip, Luke."

The meeting was called to order. After the minutes were read and approved, Tessa reported that Natalie would be available during the first two weeks in August. She was going over a tentative timeline to help with the date selection when Mr. Owens interrupted her.

"I'm still not convinced we should have the festival this year," he said.

"We have the commitment of Natalie Upman," Helen said.

He nodded. "I'm aware of that. But we're being asked to make some investments here that may just cost us a lot of money without seeing a lot of income."

"You have to spend money to make money," Tessa said, using a favorite expression of one of her business professors.

Mr. Owens swung his attention to her. "You sound awfully free with other people's money."

His vehemence startled her. "I'm making my own contribution."

He snorted. "I just don't think the town is ready for this." He lifted his hands, gesturing to the rest of them. "I'm not against the festival idea. I just think we should wait until next year."

Luke started to rise and she waved her hand under the table, motioning for him to wait. She had to do this herself.

She leaned forward, both hands pressed firmly on the

table. "Arthur," she said, stressing his first name and fixing him with a steady stare. "I know we don't have a lot of time for preparations. It would be great to have a year or at least a few more months to get ready. But we can do this." She smiled at the others. "We have a lot of talent in this town. In this room," she emphasized, standing up and waving her hand around the table. "This doesn't have to be a big event. Just something to draw people downtown."

"I agree with Tessa," Mabel said. "Would this be a good time to make a motion?" she asked Helen.

Helen nodded. "Then I move that we have the first annual Durant Founders Day Festival on the second Saturday of August of this year," Mabel said. "And that Tessa Montgomery and Luke Hunter continue to be the co-chairs of the planning committee."

Tessa actually felt a stab of relief when Bessie seconded the motion.

"Any discussion?" Helen asked.

All eyes turned toward Arthur. He shook his head, his hands lifted shoulder high. "I think you're all making a big mistake but that's all I'm going to say."

"Then let's vote."

Only Arthur voted against the motion. The rest of the meeting passed quickly and by 8:30, the meeting was adjourned.

"Nice job." Luke walked down the hallway with her. "I didn't realize he felt that strongly against the notion."

"Thank goodness I had some advance notice," she said. "Things went more smoothly than I expected."

"Because your presentation was organized and you were very mature about the shoe incident."

She looked at him, half-expecting to see him laughing at her. "I'm sincere," he said, frustration clear in his voice.

"You didn't argue with Arthur and you didn't give him any slack. Maybe you should cut *me* a little slack and start treating me as more than your best friend's annoying older brother."

He strode off, leaving her standing in the hallway with her mouth open and her mind in tumult.

Chapter Seven

Tessa wrestled the delicate desk out of the back of her small station wagon and stepped forward cautiously with her right foot. The front of her new tennis shoe bumped against the curbing and before she could regain her balance, the desk shifted in her arms.

She stretched out her arms, closing her eyes when she didn't touch anything, and cringed, imagining hours of hard work shattering on the concrete. When no crash sounded, she opened one eye and then the other, staring in surprise at the desk securely cradled against a wide chest covered by a white cotton tee shirt. Lifting her gaze past broad shoulders, a firm jaw, and a mouth curved up in a grin, she met a pair of familiar moss green eyes. "Need some help?"

Her eyes narrowed at the amusement in his voice. Obviously things had returned to normal between her and Luke. "No, thank you." She moved forward until both feet were on stable ground and reached for the desk.

He backed up, keeping the desk just out of her range. "Come on, Tessa, don't be stubborn. You almost dropped this on the ground."

"I tripped over the curb." She took another step forward but he was quicker.

"Luke! What are you doing with Anna's desk?" Christine rushed down the steps of the house and over to the couple standing in the middle of the sidewalk.

He glanced over his shoulder. "I'm saving it, sis," he said with a grin at Tessa.

She propped both fists on her hips. "I was not going to drop it."

"Oh, yeah?" He lowered the desk when his sister reached them and turned toward the house. "Does it go in Anna's room, then?"

"Yes. And don't track in any dirt!" she called after him.

"Yes, ma'am," he called back. Even with the desk in his arms, he gave Christine a mock bow.

His sister draped an arm over Tessa's shoulders. "It's gorgeous, Tessa, even better than I imagined."

"Thanks, Christine."

She walked up the sidewalk, trying to ignore the man walking in front of them. His T-shirt was tucked into a pair of worn blue jeans and she had to admit he looked good from the back.

She deliberately turned her attention back to his sister. "Are you ready for tonight?"

"I think so." Christine bit her lower lip. "We cleaned everything yesterday and Anna spent the night with Mandy so she couldn't make a mess anywhere. She kept wanting to rearrange things in her room."

Tessa laughed and wrapped an arm around Christine's

waist, giving her a quick squeeze. "She's just making it her own."

"I know, I know. But if she could just wait until after the party . . ."

As they crossed the threshold, Tessa let out a gasp and stopped, her hand dropping to her side. "Christine, it's lovely!"

"I wanted it to be perfect today," she said simply.

Tessa spun around, taking in the sheer curtains softly billowing at the floor-to-ceiling windows, the green plants hanging just in front of them, the flower-patterned cream sofa and chairs clustered invitingly around the white-stoned fireplace. She hadn't been in the house since the night she had baby-sat Anna. Christine and Jake had been determined to have the house finished and ready for a party on Memorial Day weekend.

"It's wonderful," Tessa said. "Why in the world do you need me to help with your parents' house?"

Christine shrugged. "That's different. This was . . ." She hesitated.

"A labor of love?" Tessa suggested.

"A dream come true," Christine replied. "I had this vision in my head about the kind of house I would build if I ever had the chance. And with Jake's help"—a dreamy smile came over her face—"the reality became even better."

Tessa swiveled around slowly, taking in every shining detail. "I've never lived in a new house."

"I thought you liked history," Luke asked, coming toward them from the hallway.

"I do," she said stiffly. Even with him smiling at her, she couldn't erase the image of him striding away from her after the meeting, his broad shoulders set in an angry line.

She still didn't know how she had upset him—at least that time. And she didn't want to think about why his anger with her bothered her so much. "But I like the feel of a new house, too. The possibilities."

"It does have possibilities," he said, scuffing the toe of his running shoe over the light wood of the floor. "This would make a great track. Can't you just see Anna and her friends racing through here? Then they'd be ready for the team by the time they were in high school."

Christine nudged him with her elbow. "She doesn't need any hints like that from her uncle. Jake's bad enough." Her smile took the sting out of her words. "Since you're here, would you mind helping him in the backyard? He's setting up some chairs and tables."

Luke saluted and walked around them, whistling as he went out the door. Tessa breathed a tiny sigh of relief when the door shut behind him. "So, what can I do?" she asked briskly, turning away from the sight of his long-legged stride.

"I could use some help in the kitchen."

Tessa followed her across the living room and through an arched doorway that led to the dining room. A swinging door opened into a kitchen as airy and light as the other rooms. The bright spring sunlight flooded the room.

"The windows," Tessa said.

Christine glanced at her, a hand on the cupboard door next to the sink. "What?"

"The windows. That's what makes the difference. Your windows are wider and more open than the ones in my house. You have more light." The last time she had been in Christine's kitchen, it had been nighttime. And while it was difficult to admit, even to herself, most of her attention had been on ignoring Luke.

"I wanted lots of light." Christine took several canisters out of the cupboard and lined them up on the counter next to a mixing bowl and measuring cups. "Jake keeps grumbling that our heating bills will be horrible in the winter but I told him we would keep the curtains and shades closed on the really cold days."

"Or he could keep you warm," Tessa said with a grin.

Christine laughed. "I need to remember that one. So, are you bringing anyone tonight?"

Tessa perched on a counter stool and snitched a chocolate chip from the package. "Gary's going to meet me here since I was coming over early to help get things set up."

"Gary?" Christine carefully measured flour and poured it into the bowl. "Again?"

"Yes, Gary. Why? Do you have a problem with him?"

Christine walked across the room and opened the refrigerator, bending down so her voice was muffled by the door. "Not at all. If I hadn't already been married to Jake when you introduced us, I would probably have given you a run for your money."

"Then I'm glad you're already taken. I don't need any competition."

Christine stood up, a stick of butter in her hands, her brows puckered together. "Are things getting serious between you two?"

"No, we're just friends." Tessa wrapped her heels around the rungs of her stool and watched Christine mix the ingredients together. She thought about mentioning his kiss but she still wasn't sure what it meant. Or if it meant anything. "We're both too busy with our work to think about settling down yet."

"You don't want to wait too long."

"I knew it would happen." Tessa swiped a fingerful of

batter and licked it off, grinning at her friend's suddenly wide-eyed look. Christine might not have a devious bone in her body but she wasn't buying the innocent act at all.

"What do you mean?"

"Once you were happily married, I knew you'd want to pair everybody else up."

Christine moved the bowl out of Tessa's reach. "Okay, so sue me. I just want you to be as happy as I am. Is that a crime?"

"No." Tessa reached over and gave her a quick hug around the shoulders. "But if you and Mandy start ganging up on me, I won't have a chance." Her eyes narrowed. "You've been making plans, haven't you?"

"Not exactly plans . . ." Christine's voice trailed off and she pressed her lips together, her eyes dancing.

"Of course, you have." Tessa slipped off the stool, hands fisted on her hips, glad she hadn't said a thing about the kiss. They'd have her married before the evening was over. "You better be careful. I know a good lawyer."

Christine laughed and dropped spoonfuls of batter on a pan. "We're not going to do anything. Except hope," she said when Tessa let out a snort of disbelief. "Come on, Tessa, admit it, wouldn't you like to get married?"

Oh, yes, she thought. The longing that had taken root days earlier had been steadily growing within her. But Christine had matchmaker written all over her face. Her friends might think she was possessive about her shop. That paled to nothing when compared to how she felt about her love life.

But she couldn't voice any of this to Christine.

"Sometime, sure," she said in a noncommital voice. "But I'm busy with the shop, redoing Mom and Dad's house, and now your folks' place. Besides, I haven't met the right man yet." *I don't think,* she added silently.

She leaned against the counter and stared out the window, idly watching Luke and Jake set up tables and chairs around the backyard. "Had you planned on getting married before you met Jake?"

"No," Christine conceded in a low voice.

A shout from outside diverted Tessa from Christine's comment and she squinted, trying to focus in the bright afternoon sun. Christine's husband stood in front of a small shed, a lawn chair in his hand. He was laughing, his head tossed back, and then he jabbed a finger at Luke.

The late-afternoon sun glinted on Luke's hair, turning the brown strands a burnished gold. A few tendrils curled on his forehead, damp from his exertions. He had taken off his shirt and the muscles of his back and shoulders flexed as he finished unfolding the chair in his hands

Tessa caught her breath at the picture Luke made, feeling suddenly sixteen again. He had been home from college that summer and one day when she had been visiting Christine, he had raced into the house from a run, his shirt in his hand and his skin slick with perspiration. All her budding hormones had burst toward the surface.

Until he reminded her, with a light finger flick under her chin, that he didn't have time for little girls.

Disgusted at herself, she started to turn her head toward Christine again and then paused, intrigued as Luke grabbed the chair out of Jake's hands and dropped it on the ground. With a low growl, Jake wrapped his arms around Luke's waist and tossed him to the grass next to the chair. Luke's leg snaked around Jake's knees and then they were both wrestling over the freshly mowed lawn.

She chewed on her lower lip, torn between leaving them

alone and Christine's concern about the coming party. Her loyalty to Christine won. "Um, Christine, you might want to look out the window."

Christine glanced at her and then outside. "Honestly!" She leaned forward until her nose was pressed against the screen of the open window. "Jake! Luke! Cut it out! We only have two hours until everybody gets here."

The two men ignored her, rolling over and over the grass, first Jake on top and then Luke. Blades of grass stuck to Jake's T-shirt and Luke's bare back, their hair, their arms. Christine gave an exasperated sigh and wiping her hands on a dish cloth, stomped toward the door, throwing it open before she marched across the backyard.

Tessa leaned her elbows on the window sill, grinning at the sight of two men rolling around on the ground like a couple of children. And she had taken Luke's advice on how to be grown-up!

Christine reached them and bent down, separating them with a hard push on each of their shoulders. "What's the matter with you two?"

"We're just having fun." Jake leaped to his feet and wrapped his arms around her waist, dipping her halfway to the ground before kissing her on the mouth with a smack loud enough to be heard in the kitchen.

Luke lay on the ground, one elbow propping him up, watching them.

"Jake!" Christine sounded upset but she spoiled the effect with a sputtering laugh when he kissed her again.

"Enough." Shaking her head and laughing, she pushed at his chest until he finally released her. "Come on, we have company coming in just a little bit." She reached down to help Luke to his feet.

With a fluid motion, he pulled her on top of him, tickling

her as she begged for mercy. "Luke, stop it. Jake! Help!" She giggled.

"Now you want me to touch you," Jake grumbled good-naturedly, tugging her out of Luke's reach and brushing grass and leaves from her hair.

She smoothed down her apron and then frowned at them, her hands on her hips. "No more monkey business," Tessa heard her say. "We have a lot to do." She had her nose in the air but the corners of her mouth twitched.

Jake brushed a light hand over Christine's shoulder and Tessa shivered, amazed at how much emotion could be shown with such a small gesture. "Don't you love it when she gets all bossy?" he asked Luke.

"You wouldn't love it if you'd grown up with it all your life." Luke stood up and dusted off his jeans. "Give me a woman who knows her place any day."

Tessa's humor at the silly by-play disappeared and she turned away from the window. Christine came into the kitchen. "Now what were you saying about getting married and settling down?" she asked quietly while Christine washed her hands.

"So they didn't help my argument." Christine dried her hands on a towel and leaned against the counter, a small smile playing around her lips. "It was all Luke's fault, you know. He probably said something that upset Jake."

Tessa didn't doubt it. Her blood still bubbled over the comment he had made while Christine was coming in. Just when she thought she finally understood him, he did or said something that reminded her how little they had in common.

A woman's place! What did he think this was, the Dark Ages?

How much proof did she need? she thought as they assembled sandwiches and baked cookies. Since the first time she had walked into the Hunters' house during her kindergarten year, Luke had done nothing but torment her. Either he was tugging on her braid or hiding somewhere so he could jump out at her or calling her "munchkin." They might have to work together on the festival but as soon as August rolled around, she would make plans to stay as far away from Luke as possible.

"How's Anna doing?" she asked, turning her thoughts away from him.

"She seems to be doing fine." Christine opened the oven and took out a pan of crisp chocolate-chip cookies. Their fresh smell wafted through the kitchen. "She loves Mom and Dad and she's been staying with them while I work. Luke promised to take her canoeing this summer and she's driving me crazy asking me when."

Tessa grinned. "That should be an experience. For both of them."

"What will be?" Luke asked, opening the kitchen door. He wiped his chest and forehead with his shirt as he entered the room in front of Jake.

"Christine said you're taking Anna canoeing this summer," Tessa said.

"Yup. Should be fun." He reached out and ruffled her hair. "Why don't you come with us?"

She ducked away from his hand and he grinned, his eyes crinkling at the corners. "Thanks a lot," she muttered, tucking the curls he had loosened back into her braid.

"Why do you always wear your hair pulled back like that?" he asked, tugging on the ends so that her head was tipped backward for a moment before he released her. "If you're going to keep it long, why not let people see it?

Long hair drives men wild, you know." He waggled his eyebrows.

"As if you needed another reason to be wild."

She turned her back on him and opened cupboards at random, searching for a cup. Without warning, she found herself trapped against his chest, his arms resting on the counter on either side of her.

"Are you calling me wild?" he murmured in her ear.

She told herself it was the shock that was making her heart pound. "I saw you outside with Jake." She pushed against the steel bands of his arms.

"And . . . ?"

The drawn-out question ruffled the hair around her ears. She swallowed, refusing to let him see that she was bothered by him. "And you weren't acting like a highly respected high school teacher," she said primly.

He gave a shout of laughter and raised one hand, reaching over her head for a glass. Filling it at the sink, he drank it down with one gulp, his head tipped back, the strong muscles of his throat moving with each swallow.

She stepped away from him, her heart still pounding, and pressed a hand to her chest. What was the matter with her? Luke had been giving her a hard time for years. Why did she keep having these strange reactions with him?

"Tessa," Christine said, breaking into her thoughts. "I need to check on something with Jake. I'll be right back," and she left before Tessa could even respond.

She was aware of Luke behind her, opening the dishwasher and loading the empty water glasses onto the top shelf. "What else can I do?" he asked Tessa, turning around.

Put on your shirt, she wanted to say. Her heart still hadn't slowed down. She scooted a tray of sandwiches toward the center of the table and fiddled with the snacks Christine had already arranged. "Those dishes in the sink need to go in the dishwasher, too," she said, not looking at him.

He hummed under his breath, the sound punctuated by the clink of the dishes as he loaded them.

The door snapped closed behind her and she could hear him pushing the buttons. *Just like he's always pushing mine,* she thought with a flash of insight. *But I'm not going to let him bug me this time.*

"Now what?" He reached over and helped himself to a small sandwich from the top of the pile.

"Go take your shower," she ordered, smacking the back of his hand. She was relieved when her heart didn't react at the touch. It was just the surprise of being cornered like that, she thought in relief.

He popped the sandwich in his mouth. "I don't mind helping."

"We're done." She moved away from him. The aftershave he had used for as long as she could remember, mingled with the odor of newly cut grass, was doing funny things to her. "Go before Christine comes back in here. She doesn't need to worry that her guests will arrive while her brother's standing in the kitchen all sweaty."

"Yes, ma'am." He gave her another one of his salutes and sauntered down the hallway.

Breathing a sigh of relief when he went down the hall, she picked up the cookie batter and focused all her attention on dropping even spoonfuls on the pan.

Hours later, she leaned against a corner of the living room wall and sipped a glass of iced tea, watching half the community wander around, laughing, chatting, and munching on the food she had helped prepare. Christine stood near the front door with Jake and Anna, greeting the guests and accepting their compliments on the house.

A small blond woman paused next to Tessa, a plate filled with sandwiches, chips and pickles in each hand.

"Eating for two, Abby?" Tessa asked.

"Don't even suggest such a thing," Abby retorted with a slight shudder. "I'm still not getting any sleep at night."

"Tim keeping you up?"

"Funny, Tessa. Tyler still hasn't decided if he wants to sleep through the night."

"You wanted children, Abby. This is only the beginning." Tessa grinned around her glass of tea.

"You just wait, Tessa Montgomery. One of these days you'll be moaning from lack of sleep and we won't give you a speck of sympathy."

The image of a small child took shape within her mind. A little boy, with brown tousled curls, kissed by the sun, and mischievous green eyes . . .

She blinked and gave herself a mental shake. "Well, it won't be anytime soon," she said banishing the child to the farthest corner of her mind. "Need a husband first."

She lifted a hand when Abby opened her mouth. "Don't even think about it. I've already discussed the matter with Christine."

"We can hope," Abby grumbled.

Tessa laughed and watched Abby maneuver through the crowd. She stopped in front of her husband, seated on one corner of the crowded couch, and handed him a plate. Before she could move, he snagged her around the waist and plopped her in his lap, holding his plate out of danger of being spilled when she landed.

Abby scowled at him as she tried to balance her plate

but even from her distance, Tessa could see the love that lit her eyes.

"Tessa," a deep voice rumbled quietly into her ear.

She jumped and tea splashed out of her glass and onto the floor. "Now look what you made me do, Luke." She bent over and scrubbed away the spot with her napkin.

He took the glass out of her hand and placed it on a low table next to them. "Just in case you get nervous again," he said with a grin.

Warm color flushed into her cheeks. She had been so engrossed in the love play going on between Abby and Tim, she hadn't realized anyone else was around. And with the image of that baby peeking out of the far corners of her mind at her . . .

"I'm not nervous," she said quickly. "You just startled me."

She straightened her shoulders. His eyes weren't that green. And they didn't look mischievous, at least not right now.

In fact, they had a flat, dull look to them. "What did you want?" she asked.

"You had a phone call."

Her heart slowed. With her parents both traveling in her father's truck, she lived with the unspoken fear that she would receive a phone call telling her they had been in an accident. "Where's a phone?"

He lifted both hands and rested them on her shoulders, squeezing gently. "Relax. It's not your mom and dad."

She shifted away from his touch, uncomfortable he had read so much into her response. She had never even told Christine that she worried about her parents. "Who is it then?"

"Gary." Luke snagged a sandwich from a nearby plate and chomped on it, watching the crowd.

She resisted the urge to punch him on the shoulder. Was she going to have to drag the message out word by word? "Is he still on the phone?" she asked carefully.

Luke swallowed and turned toward her. "No, he just left a message. Said he'd be over in about an hour."

Tessa felt only a small twinge of regret that Gary would be late. Without him, she was free to move around the crowd. And after her conversation with Christine, she didn't like the thought that others might be making serious plans about her and Gary.

But she didn't plan to share any of that with Luke.

"Hey, Tessa, hi!"

Tessa swung away from Luke with a smile on her face that widened when she saw her greeter. "Seth!"

He grabbed her around the middle and lifted her off her feet before planting a loud kiss on her cheek. "When did you get back?" she asked, her feet back on the floor.

"Last night. I couldn't miss little sister's party, could I?"

Tessa pressed her hands against his chest and eased back until she could see him clearly. "You look great."

"Thanks." His eyes traveled over her from head to toe and then back to her face. "You're not so bad yourself."

"How about me, little brother?" Luke asked, directing their attention back to him.

Seth favored his older brother with a cursory glance. "No improvement," he said with such a forlorn tone that Tessa couldn't help giggling.

Luke gave her a sour frown that didn't reach his eyes. The bantering between the brothers was as familiar to her as the friendly rivalry that had always been part of their relationship. Fortunately Luke had excelled in track and field while Seth had found a position on the soccer team.

She looped her arm through Seth's. "Have you had a tour yet?"

"No. I just walked in and grabbed a few sandwiches. It's taken me several minutes just to make my way across the room to you."

"Come on, I'll do the honors. Christine won't mind."

While they walked through the various rooms, she asked him about the trip he had taken, aware as they talked that Luke was tagging along. Seth might have teased her when they were younger but since she had returned from college, their friendship had matured.

Not that she would ever consider him for a boyfriend, she thought in surprise as he checked out the detail on the desk she had refinished for Anna. He had just finished a vivid description about the scuba diving he had enjoyed in the Caribbean and invited her to go with him sometime. She had laughingly turned him down, saying that he should take someone besides his sister's best friend to such a romantic spot.

She couldn't imagine their relationship going beyond the pleasant camaraderie they now shared. He was funny, they shared a lot of good times, but when he wasn't around, she didn't think about him that much.

Which wasn't the case with Luke. He kept creeping into her thoughts, causing her to wonder what he was doing, what he was thinking. He had followed them through the rooms, adding his comments to hers, giving information she hadn't known.

So why do you keep thinking about Luke in that way? she asked herself. *He's Christine's brother, too.*

Which is why I can't date him. Or even let him know I'm

interested, she reminded herself. *If I do, and things don't work out, I could lose one of my best friends.*

"You should go down there," Seth said, breaking into her thoughts. "Even if it's not with me. You'd love it."

Luke leaned against the door, his arms folded across his chest. "If she wants hot weather, she doesn't need to fly anywhere."

She turned away from the confusion Luke created in her and gave Seth a sweet smile. "It's not just the temperature, is it?"

"No. It's the atmosphere, the ocean breeze, the swaying palm trees. . . ." He sniffed, closing his eyes, and sighed.

"Give me a good Missouri summer anytime," Luke said. "I don't need to go somewhere fancy for my vacation."

"That's because you have no imagination," Tessa tossed over her shoulder.

She didn't have any warning. Luke scooped her up and carried her across the room, dropping her on the single bed from shoulder high. She bounced a few times before she rolled to the edge of the bed and jumped to her feet, moving several inches away from him.

"No imagination?" he asked, grinning at her. "Who do you think dreamed up all our plans when we were growing up?"

She smoothed down her blouse. "That didn't take much imagination," she said in a haughty tone, her nose in the air as she walked back to the door. "Just somebody ornery."

His laughter followed her down the hallway. What was he doing to her? One minute she was imagining children that looked like him and the next, she felt like a child again, being teased by the big brother of her best friend.

She slipped into the kitchen, needing a few moments to collect her thoughts. "But that's the best way," she muttered under her breath. "Just keep thinking of him as Christine's big brother. Otherwise, what are you going to do? You don't want to marry him, do you?"

She blinked and stared out the window. A few small groups clustered around the chairs Luke and Jake had finally managed to set up. She rested her hands on the edge of the sink, taking slow, easy breaths.

Marry Luke? Where did that idea keep coming from? She hadn't even kissed him yet!

And you aren't going to, she reminded herself. *You and Luke are friends, nothing more. You've been thrown together a lot recently due to circumstances but once the festival is over and you finish redecorating his folks' house, you won't be around each other that much.*

Gary's coming in a little while and you'll see he's more the kind of man you want to be around. If you were ready to get married. Just think about him.

Confident her emotions didn't show on her face, she picked up a relish tray, balancing it on her forearm, and then picked up two trays of sandwiches.

"Need some help carrying that?" her nemesis asked from behind her.

Now was a good time to put her strategy into practice. She closed her eyes and took a deep breath, slowly counting to ten, dredging up Gary's face. She opened her eyes and glanced over her shoulder. Luke stood by the kitchen door that led to the living room, his hands stretched toward her load.

She backed away from him, edging around the table and toward the swinging door. "I'm fine."

Turning sideways, she used her hip to push the door open

but it didn't budge. Surprised, she gave it another thump with her hip. The door moved an inch and then, as if in slow motion, swung back toward her and the trays, sending all of them into the air and over Luke.

Chapter Eight

Pickle juice trickled down Luke's face. A piece of roast beef stuck to his shoulder, the mustard acting as glue. An olive sat on the top of his head and as she watched, it rolled over his forehead and down his nose before sailing onto the floor.

"Oh, Luke, I'm sorry." She pressed a hand to her mouth, biting on her lips to hide her grin.

"Not a problem." He brushed lettuce off his chest and stepped over the mess to the sink.

The door opened a fraction of an inch and Christine peeked around. "Is anything the matter?" She gasped when she saw the food on the floor. "What happened?"

"You pushed the door open when I was trying to go out," Tessa explained. She bent down and gingerly picked up a squished sandwich, dropping it on the empty tray.

Christine opened the door wider and tiptoed over the

food littering the floor. "I told Jake we needed a window in it."

"No, it was my fault." Tessa scooped up carrots and celery and plopped them unceremoniously on the now-ruined sandwiches. "I shouldn't have carried so much."

Luke shot her an "I told you so" look over his shoulder. She gave him a tight smile and turned back to her work.

"Why were you out here anyway? You're not the hostess."

"No, I'm a friend of the hostess." She picked up the trays and carried them over to the sink. She reached around Luke to get the roll of paper towels. She was not about to say that she had taken refuge in the kitchen because of him. That would only add to the problem.

"Well, it's not your job," Christine continued. "I hope you didn't get anything on your clothes."

"I don't know why she would," Luke grumbled, scrubbing at his shirt. "She threw it all at me."

Christine glanced at Tessa. They stared at each other a moment and then fell into each other's arms, laughing until Tessa had tears coming down her cheeks.

"I'm glad you find this amusing," Luke muttered. He marched over to them and pointed to his stained shirt. "Look at this. It's ruined."

"Oh, don't be a baby," Christine managed, brushing at her eyes. "It'll wash out."

Pulling the material away from his body, he frowned at the dark spots covering the tan design. "Are you sure?"

"Oh, come on, Luke," Tessa said, grabbing his hand and leading him back to the sink. She found a clean rag in one of the drawers and dampened it.

She sponged at a spot near his waist and worked her way

up the shirt, lifting the stains easily until she reached one near the V-neck. Resting her hand on his shoulder, she scrubbed a little harder until she felt the steady thud of his heartbeat under her fingers.

Her hand faltered and she tightened her grip around the rag. His shoulder was warm and she could feel the strong muscles through the thin material.

Swallowing, she kept her head averted from him. The spot refused to come out of the material. Carefully loosening her hold on his shoulder, she dropped her hand to her side and stepped away from him.

"This one won't come out," she murmured, unable to look him in the face.

"Which one?" He tipped his head down and studied the recalcitrant blemish. "I guess I could live with one."

"Or we could find you one of Jake's shirts," Christine put in. "You're about the same size. Then you could soak the shirt."

"That sounds good."

Before Tessa had a moment to react, he stripped off the shirt and dropped it into the sink. He smelled fresh from his shower. She took a quick step backward and almost tripped over a chair.

"Come on," Christine said, her attention on Luke. "We can go down the back hallway and nobody will see you without a shirt." He followed her out of the room, still muttering under his breath as they walked.

Tessa ran warm water in the sink and dropped the trays in to soak. *So Luke has broad shoulders and looks good without his shirt,* she chided herself. *You've seen him like that before.* Just a little bit ago, in fact.

Doesn't make any difference anyway. He's still your best

friend's brother. You don't want to muddy your relationship with her.

More in control of herself, she poured a glass of water and drank it down quickly, feeling her system shift back to normal. Gary should be arriving soon. Pasting a smile on her face, she picked up a single tray of snacks and carefully carried them into the living room.

Twilight had blanketed the house and the lamps were turned on by the time Gary arrived. "Sorry I'm late." Gary joined her on the couch, stretching his legs out as far as he could. "I had to go to St. Louis again this weekend and I just made it back."

His dark eyes looked tired and lines creased his forehead. "We don't have to stay much longer," she offered, glad of an excuse to go home early. Christine would understand if she didn't stay and help clean up. She'd probably start making a guest list for the wedding, Tessa thought with a flash of ironic humor.

Gary snared a drink from the tray sitting on the low table beside them. "No, I need this, to forget about work for a while. Besides, I'm starving."

"Should I get you a plate of food?" Luke was standing near the array of food, talking to several friends, but she could easily walk around the other side of the table.

"Not yet. I'll get something in a little while." He leaned back and rested his head on the back of the couch, surveying the crowd. "So, what's been going on?"

"Mostly visiting. Do you want a tour?"

"Later." He turned his head toward her. "Any good gossip?"

She laughed. "Since when have you cared about gossip?"

"You never know. I might find something that would lead to a client."

Her laugh bubbled out again. He didn't need to go looking for clients. Ever since his arrival last fall in Durant, people had been almost tripping over themselves to hire a lawyer who didn't already know everything about their family and their situations. Until she started seeing him, she hadn't realized how many people in Durant used a lawyer.

Not that he told her much. Confidentiality was a prime factor in his success and she appreciated that, especially since she didn't like having her every action weighed and measured by the community.

They talked quietly, their voices mingling with the others in the room. She could hear the fatigue in his voice but he rejected her repeated offer to leave early. "I'm not that tired," he told her.

A shadow fell over them. She glanced up and saw Luke standing in front of them, his legs braced slightly apart. "Hi, Templar," he said gruffly. "Glad you could make it."

Gary extended his hand to Luke. After they shook hands, Luke tucked his hands into his back pockets and continued to stand in front of them.

"Luke could help you," Tessa put in, confused by Luke's wary stance. If she didn't know better, she would think he was upset by Gary's appearance.

"What?" Luke asked.

"Gary runs," she said, glancing between the two men. "He wants to know some good running trails. He hasn't found very many yet, except around town, and I thought you would know some longer routes that don't have much traffic."

Luke settled on her arm of the couch. "Depends on how far you want to go."

While they talked about running, Tessa studied both of them. Gary's dark hair was brushed away from his forehead in a sleek style that provided a frame for his face. Only the slight bend in his nose stopped his face from being perfect, a fact that Tessa thought made him look more interesting.

Luke's features were almost as familiar as her own. She would probably have been able to describe him clearly enough for a police artist to complete a picture of him.

Her eyes narrowed a fraction. If she was describing him, she would find it difficult not to mention the ready smile that was usually on his lips or the constant twinkle in his eyes. Now, though his voice was pleasant and he was talking easily with Gary, the smile seemed forced, as if he would rather be anywhere than sitting with them, and his eyes were more intense than normal.

She focused on the conversation, ready to break in if things became uncomfortable for Gary. "You think old Highway 14 is the best route?" Gary asked.

Luke nodded, his arm rubbing against her shoulder. "Since the new highway came in, that road is hardly used by anyone. You'll have to watch out for some major potholes, though."

He grinned and Tessa relaxed. She had been letting her imagination run away with her thoughts earlier. Catherine's son would never be rude to a guest.

"Thanks." Gary stretched and twisted his neck from side to side. "Tessa, I think I will take you up on that earlier offer."

Luke tensed by her side and she slanted him an assessing glance before giving her attention to Gary. "The tour?"

He nodded. "A short one. And then I need to get home.

You're right, I am tired. A few more minutes and I'll be asleep on this very comfortable couch."

He stood up and reached for Tessa's hand, helping her to her feet. "Thanks, Hunter, for the suggestion," he said. "I'll try it out tomorrow if I get a good night's sleep."

Luke lazily rolled to his feet next to them. Tessa had never seen the two men next to each other and she was surprised that Luke was the taller by several inches. Gary's lean build made him seem taller but he was probably only a few inches taller than her own five-foot-ten.

"We can start in the kitchen," Tessa said, weaving through several small clusters of visiting guests.

Luke fell into step on her other side. "Jake and Christine have worked hard with the place," he said.

She stared at him, willing him to look her way. When he did, she gave him a quick nod of her head away from them. Luke met her expression with only a slight widening of his eyes before he leaned around her to speak to Gary again. "If you're ever in the market for a house, Jake is the guy. I couldn't believe he could get things done so soon."

"He did have a vested interest," Tessa managed. Did he think she needed a chaperone in his own sister's house?

Luke didn't budge from her side during the entire tour. He added tidbits of information to everything she said, lingering in several of the rooms and regaling them with stories about the events that had taken place during the months while the house was being built. At least he was being entertaining, she thought, bewildered by his persistence.

"Christine made most of the decorating decisions," he said when Gary pointed out the pleasant features of the back bedroom that would be Jake's home office. "Tessa gave some advice. Hey, did you know she's working with us to do some remodeling on our parents' house?"

Tessa sent a quick glance around. His parents had been part of the crowd gathered in the living room earlier. "I thought it was a secret," she whispered.

"From Mom and Dad." He smiled at Gary. "But I can trust you, can't I, Gary?"

Gary nodded, giving him a strange look. "Sure, Luke."

Tessa stared at Luke. What was the matter with him? Not that he wasn't being friendly. But his constant talking, his long stories . . . Totally out of character.

He walked with them back to the front door. "Thanks, Luke," she said in a firm voice, hoping he would take the hint.

He glanced from her to Gary and then back to her before slapping a hand against his forehead. "Am I stupid or what? I bet you two wanted to be alone and here I am, following you around like some demented tour guide." He backed up a pace. "Listen, it was good to see you again, Gary. Maybe we could take a run together sometime." He melted into the remaining crowd.

"I'm sorry about that," Tessa murmured as they walked out the front door. Several others had decided to enjoy the light spring breeze and were wandering around the front yard.

Gary caught her hand and squeezed it gently. "It's okay. I think he wonders about my intentions."

She was glad the shadowy light covered the telltale blush spreading up her neck and over her cheeks. "It's just that we've known each other for a long time and he's been in the habit of watching out for me and his sister," she explained in a rush. Not that Luke usually cared about what she did, but it was the best excuse she could offer Gary.

Over the soft glare of the streetlights that were strategically placed along the street and the treetops, she caught the reflected light of the first evening stars. The lot Jake had developed was at the edge of town and provided both the privacy of the country with the convenience of the city. She hadn't been surprised when she heard that Mandy and Greg had recently bought a lot in the same area and knew that Jake was already making progress on their new house.

Gary interrupted her musings by bringing her fingers to his lips and lightly kissing them. He dropped her hand and covered a loud yawn before she had time to barely register the kiss. "I'm sorry," he said, a rueful grin in his eyes.

"You need to go home and get some sleep. You've looked tired all night." She smoothed a hand over his forehead, brushing back a lock of hair the breeze had dislodged.

"I don't want to spoil the party for you."

Luke had already done that with his interference, she thought. She wouldn't be surprised to see him peering out the window at them. "You won't. I'll stay and help clean up for a while and then go home myself."

He hid another yawn. "If you're sure . . ."

"Go home." She gave him a little push toward the line of cars parked along the street. "How can you win cases if you fall asleep on your feet?"

"I'll make this up for you later. How about dinner tomorrow night?"

She started to agree and then stopped. She was meeting Christine to look over paint samples for the Hunters' house. They only had a few weeks before Paul and Catherine left on their cruise. "I'm busy tomorrow. But the next night would be fine."

He shook his head. "I have a meeting that night." Another yawn slipped out. He bent and lightly brushed his lips over hers. "I'll call you at work tomorrow and we can coordinate our schedules."

She waited until he was at his car, waved good-bye to him, and then returned to the house. If it weren't for Christine, she would go home. She was in no mood to face Luke.

He didn't disappoint her. She had barely entered the house when he materialized at her side. "Where's your boyfriend?"

She slowly counted to ten. "Gary went home. He just came back from a quick trip to St. Louis and he's tired."

"So he just left you here?"

This time she counted to fifteen before she was calm enough to face him. "I came on my own, remember, Luke? Gary knew I planned to help Christine clean up."

He shrugged. "Seems like an odd date to me."

She swung around, ignoring the buzz in her ears that said she needed to wait before she opened her mouth. "If you have a problem with me seeing Gary, then say so. Otherwise, stop all these snide innuendoes."

His brows drew together in a puzzled frown. "I don't have a problem with you seeing Gary."

She took a step back, puzzled. "Then what are all these cracks about our dating?"

His eyes twinkled and one corner of his mouth curved upward. "I have a problem with *him* dating *you.*"

She barely restrained herself from taking a swing at him. She was not a violent person. Her friends and business acquaintances would be amazed to know she even considered raising her voice. Pivoting away from him, she contented herself with a tiny sniff and stalked into the living room.

Luke stayed away from her the rest of the evening, which gave her some source of peace. She was aware of him, catching his laugh in the middle of a conversation, hearing his deep voice raised in good-byes as people left. Seth invited her onto the patio and she willingly followed him, determined to ignore Luke and his weird sense of humor as much as possible.

Tessa carried an armload of plates into the kitchen. "That's it," she said, adding them to the pile next to the sink.

"I hope so." Luke lifted soapy hands from the dishwater and groaned. "My fingers are shriveling up."

She put the last of the leftover snacks into the refrigerator. "Too bad it's not your vocal cords. You've done nothing but gripe. If somebody didn't know you, they'd think you really did hate to work."

"Hey, don't blow my cover!"

He swiped a dishtowel toward her but she nimbly jumped aside, grinning at his scowl.

Her earlier irritation with him had disappeared as quickly as it had flared up. She could never stay upset with Luke for long. She swung around and marched back into the living room, the kitchen door rhythmically swinging behind her.

"Eh, Tessa, does this look right?"

She turned around at Seth's question. He was critically eyeing a pillow on the couch. She stepped forward and twitched a corner into place. "Looks good. I can't believe the house was filled with people only an hour ago."

"We don't have many rowdy friends," Jake said, coming into the room, his arm twined around Christine's shoulders. "Most of them do clean up after themselves."

Tessa chuckled. "Anna asleep?" Seth asked.

Christine nodded. "I was afraid she'd be up all night. She was so excited and she had so much soda."

Jake kissed the top of her head. "She was just as excited

to be sleeping in her new room. You've really created a home for her. For us," he murmured, cradling her against his chest with both arms.

Tessa felt as if she were intruding. She glanced at Seth and he nodded, getting her unspoken message immediately. He gave a huge yawn, clapping his hand over his mouth.

"Sorry," he said when Christine and Jake looked at him. "Sleep sounds great. I'm still a little jet-lagged."

Tessa edged toward the kitchen. "I need to go, too. I'll just grab my sweater and be on my way."

"I've got it right here." Luke pushed through the swinging door, her sweater over his arm. He held it while she slipped her arms into it, holding her hair off her neck.

Her skin heated at the intimate gesture. He did that so naturally, she thought, like they'd done it before.

He stepped away from her and she buttoned the front of the sweater to give herself something to do. "Great party, sis." He kissed Christine's cheek and nodded at Jake. "We'll get out of your way."

The two brothers flanked Tessa as they walked out of the house. Jake and Christine waved to them from the front porch and then went back inside, clicking off the outside light once the three reached the protective halo of the street light near their cars.

Tessa paused next to her car and hugged Seth around the waist. "I'm glad you made it. Christine didn't say anything but I know she was afraid you wouldn't be here."

"I always planned to make it back in time." He glanced toward the house. "Anna looks happy."

"She's doing better," Luke said quietly.

Tessa slanted a glance toward him.

"What?" he asked quietly.

"I—it's—" She broke off, unsure what to say to him.

"It's not all fun and games with me at school," he said carefully.

She nodded, unable to look at him. He had totally mis-understood her look. No matter how frustrated he made her, she would never make the mistake of thinking that he wasn't a compassionate teacher. She knew that he went out of his way for his students and the athletes he coached. "I know that. It's just that the thought of Anna, her mom and dad . . ."

A lump formed in her throat and she suddenly had an urge to call her own parents, to let them know how much she cared for them. She couldn't imagine how she would have survived if they had died when she was little, even if she had been fortunate enough to have a supportive family circle like Anna now had.

She dug in her purse for her car keys. "Good night," she said tightly, walking quickly toward her car.

Footsteps sounded behind her and a hand gently touched her shoulder. "Are you okay?" Luke asked.

How could she admit she wanted to hear her mother's voice? After all her talk of independence, he would tease her incessantly. His ridicule was the last thing she wanted.

She didn't want to analyze that strange thought. She just wanted to go home, to the comfort and security of her own house.

"I'm fine. Just tired." She bent down, her key in her hand. Her vision blurred and she found it difficult to find the keyhole.

"Let me."

His voice was gentle and she swallowed hard to keep her tears from falling. She didn't argue when he leaned down and took the keys from her hand. She was just tired. It had nothing to do with Luke being kind.

The button clicked up and Luke opened her door, holding it so she could slide into the seat. "Are you sure you're okay?"

She nodded, her eyes on the steering wheel. He leaned against her door and his shadow fell across her lap, a large, comforting shape. "I could follow you home, make sure you get there okay."

She blinked back another bout of tears. Why couldn't he be his usual, teasing self? This considerate Luke, on top of her loneliness, was almost too much. "I've been driving myself home alone for a long time, Luke." She stuck her key in the ignition, determined to get away before she broke down completely.

He stepped away from the car. "I didn't mean to offend you."

She felt a momentary flash of guilt. He was only being considerate, looking out for her. He would probably do the same thing for Christine.

The thought didn't dispel her mood. "You didn't offend me," she said.

"Why don't you call and let me know you got home safely?"

She glanced at him. The streetlight glinted on his hair, the dark intensified his eyes. Her fingers tightened on the steering wheel and she licked her lips nervously.

"Good grief," Seth said from behind him. "Tessa's a big girl. She doesn't need to check in with you."

Luke stepped back and she breathed easier. She had forgotten Seth was there. She favored him with a wide smile. "You're right, I'll be fine." She tugged the door closed, shutting herself into the cocoon of her car, away from Luke's disturbing presence. Waving at them both, she started the engine and drove toward her end of town.

The streets were quiet, most of the town already settled for the night. A bat flew over the hood of her car, its wings spread as it searched for prey. Two eyes glittered in the beam of her headlight and then disappeared as a cat slithered into the bushes.

Stars twinkled overhead and she relaxed, welcoming the solitude. The party had been fun and she had enjoyed seeing her friends, sharing in Christine's happiness, but she had also felt isolated several times. She tried pinning the unsettled feeling on Gary's limited appearance and yet she knew that wasn't the real reason.

She still hadn't sorted out her feelings when she arrived home. She slipped the car into its place in the garage and went into the house, clicking on lights as she walked through the rooms. If her neighbors looked out their windows, they would think she was having her own party but she was certain most of them were safely tucked into their beds.

She carried the portable phone into the living room, carefully making her way around the furniture stacked in the middle of the floor. Once at the sofa, she kicked off her shoes and curled her feet under her, settling against the back cushions before she dialed her parents' cell phone number.

She chewed on her lower lip, listening to the rings echo over the line. As the tenth ring faded away, she moved the receiver from her ear and raised her finger to punch it off. A soft "hello" had her pressing the phone back against her ear.

"Mom?"

"Tessa, is that you? I'm sorry I took so long to answer. I was reading on the bed and couldn't find the phone right away."

Relief at hearing her mother's voice washed over her. "It's okay. I just thought I'd see how you're doing."

"We're fine. We stopped at Aunt Sylvia's yesterday. She sent you her love and a huge box."

"Great. I just finished sorting through the last ones."

Her great-aunt had taken most of Tessa's great-grandparents' belongings to her home in Seattle after their deaths, dividing the more personal items among her three brothers. The rest had been stored in her attics and during the last few years, she had started sorting them, sending boxes of less-treasured objects to Tessa for her shop.

The couple had been one of the first families in Durant shortly after the turn of the twentieth century. Tessa had loved listening to her grandmother and great-aunt talk about their early years in the town and hearing the stories their parents had told them. She knew much of her love of history came from these two women. Walking into buildings or down streets that had been created years before by people her grandmother had known always sent a thrill through her that she had been unable to match with any other activity. She knew it was part of the reason she felt so strongly about saving the downtown.

"So, how was Seattle?" she asked, stretching out on the couch.

"Wet. We spent the night with Sylvia and she brought out the photo albums."

Tessa grinned. "I bet Dad loved that."

"He looked at a few pictures to be polite and then he went into the other room with his newspaper. Tessa . . ."

She paused and Tessa waited, wondering at her mother's uncharacteristic hesitancy. They had always been a close family. Only Tessa's desire to open her own shop and her mother's wish to travel with her father had ever been kept secret and those had quickly been shared at the appropriate time.

"Aunt Sylvia wants you to have her mother's wedding dress."

Tessa stiffened. She didn't need this right now. "Mom . . ." she began.

"You know she always expected the dress to be passed down each generation. She just thinks it would be better if you kept it instead of having it tucked away in her attic. She's afraid something might happen to her before she could get it to you."

"She's all right, isn't she?"

"She's fine. But she is getting older, Tessa."

"And so are you." Her mother didn't say the words but Tessa could almost hear them filtering their way over the airwaves. "I don't have any plans to get married right away. You told her that, didn't you?"

"Of course. That doesn't mean we can't hope."

Tessa relaxed against the sofa cushions. Her earlier panic subsided at the familiar comments. She knew what was coming, just as she knew what she would have for breakfast the next morning.

"I'd like to have grandchildren," her mother continued. "Why should Catherine have all the fun? Not that I expect them right away. You don't have to marry a man who has a child," she added. "Unless, of course, he's like Jake and he has the responsibility already. But just the thought that someday, I'd have a grandchild to dote on . . ." Her voice trailed away.

Tessa shook her head, a smile curving her lips. "You know what, Mom? Why don't you make a recording? Then when we get to this part of the conversation, I could say good-bye, turn on the tape recorder and listen to the same thing over and over without spending any money on long distance."

Her mother chuckled. "I'm sorry, honey. It's just that after visiting Sylvia, I always feel this strong family pull. Especially since she brought up the wedding dress."

Tessa understood. She had felt the same urge when she left Christine's house. A need to feel that she belonged, that someone cared about her and shared her history.

Not that she didn't love her friends. She couldn't remember when she hadn't been around Christine or Mandy or Abby. They were as much a part of her life as her parents. In some ways, possibly more. But they were starting their own families and it was only natural that they would begin drifting apart.

She visited with her mother a little longer, relaying the latest Durant news to her. They e-mailed each other while they were traveling, sending messages daily, but she knew her mother liked to hear what was going on from Tessa. "You were missed tonight," she told her mother after letting her know the health of several friends.

"Did you go with Gary?"

Tessa hesitated, reluctant to bring in her dating status after their earlier discussion. "He met me at Christine's house." She didn't mention how soon after his arrival he left.

"At least you saw him tonight."

Tessa knew her mother was referring to the many times their dates had been canceled due to one or the other's work schedule. "We're both busy, Mom."

"I know and I don't want to be a busybody but it seems to me that if you wanted to be together, you'd find the time."

She could hear her father saying something to her mother. "What did Dad say?"

"He says I should leave you alone and let you go to bed."

Tessa glanced at the mantle clock. "It's just eleven o'clock. You're not getting out of this so easily, Mom."

"A checkpoint's up ahead so I need to get off anyway. We love you."

The buzz of an empty phone echoed in her ear. Smiling and shaking her head at the constancy of her mother's meddling, she clicked off the phone and dropped it onto the coffee table, sliding down until her head rested against the arm of the sofa. Her arms crossed over her chest, she studied the ceiling, her mind mulling over their conversation.

She hadn't ruled out marriage. She could even see Gary as husband material.

Christine's earlier comments came back to her. He was an eligible bachelor, probably even more than Luke. Based on the amount of work he did, she didn't doubt he earned a respectable income.

Not that money would be an issue if she really loved the man.

She just hated being nagged into a decision. She and Gary had never even talked about future plans. When she was with him, they focused on the present, relaxing and leaving their work behind. Their times together were comfortable.

She probably should care more when their dates were canceled but she liked being on her own, working at the shop late without having to let someone know. If she didn't want to come home for supper, nibbling on carrots and peanut butter sandwiches in her office, it was no one's business but her own. If she wanted to spend her weekend traveling the back roads in search of estate auctions and sales, she could do it with a clear conscience.

The phone rang, startling her out of her thoughts. She rolled over and picked up the receiver, grinning.

"Are you going to apologize?" she asked, knowing her mother would start on her concerns all over again if she didn't say something first.

"Apologize?"

She jerked upright. "Luke?"

"Hi." His deep voice rumbled over the line. "I saw all your lights on and thought I'd see if everything is all right."

"How did you see my lights on?" She frowned, her brows puckering together. "Did you drive by my house after all?"

"Not really. I had to run an errand and it took me past your place. If everything's okay . . ."

"An errand? At this time of the night?"

"Okay, I just wanted to see if you're okay. I was worried about you."

A warm glow started in her middle and spread outward. "You don't need to be worried about me. I'm fine, really. But thank you."

"If everything's okay . . ."

She stood up and headed toward the stairs, clicking off lights as she went. "It is. If you're sitting out front, you can see that I'm on my way upstairs. Good night, Luke."

Her mind still reeling from the thought that Luke was driving around checking on her, she walked into the bathroom.

Brushing her teeth, she stared at her reflection and then grinned. Thank goodness her mother wasn't around! If she knew that Luke was checking on her daughter, she'd have the wedding dress at the cleaners by morning. She knew her mother would love nothing more than to be permanently tied to the Hunter family. She had made enough broad hints about Christine's brothers over the past few years.

"I don't want to jeopardize my friendship with Christine," she said out loud. "If it didn't work out, it would be hard to get together with her."

The argument against seeing Luke didn't sound as strong when she was facing herself in the mirror. And crawling under the covers, she wondered why she always imagined it not working out.

Chapter Nine

"What's going on with you?"

Tessa jumped. A shadow covered her desk. She swung around and found herself face to face with a scowling Abby.

Her hand pressed against her chest, she waited until her breathing was back to normal before speaking. "Hi. What are you doing here?"

Abby yanked an empty chair next to the desk and plopped herself on it. "I drew the short straw, that's what."

"What are you talking about?" Tessa closed up the catalog she had been studying, knowing she wouldn't be able to work until Abby had stated her purpose.

"Where have you been for the last month?"

"The last month? Working on the festival, redecorating my mom's house, keeping my shop doors open, hitting a few sales." She gave Abby a cautious look. New mothers were known to have odd mood swings. She didn't remem-

155

ber Abby having any when Melissa was born but maybe second children did things to a woman. "Why?"

"Because nobody's seen you." Abby crossed her arms over her chest, her brows lowered over her blue eyes.

"Christine has seen me!" she sputtered at the injustice of the accusation. "How do you think we finished her folks' house?"

She had met with Christine several times, going over plans, shopping for furniture. Luke had been noticeably absent. Christine had said that he was deferring all decisions to them and after Tessa had recovered from the initial shock of actually missing him, she had thrown herself into the project. Once Paul and Catherine had driven to the airport in Tulsa for the first leg of their trip, the Hunter children and Tessa had gone to work, finishing the decorating with a day to spare.

"Okay, Christine has seen you." Abby's expression had mellowed.

"And I've visited Mandy several times. Didn't she show you that antique bank I found for David's nursery?"

Abby nodded.

"And I've seen you here in town," Tessa added.

"So you haven't dropped completely off the face of the earth," Abby conceded.

"So why are you upset?"

"Because you've missed our last two get-togethers."

Tessa stared at her and then grabbed her daybook, flipping through the pages. She groaned. "Honest, Abby, I didn't do it on purpose. I even had them schedule the DBC meetings on the second and fourth Thursdays so I would be free on the first one."

For as long as she could remember, the four of them had been getting together once a month. Sometimes they watched a movie, sometimes they just sat around and talked. Even after the others started getting married, the monthly get-togethers continued, no matter how many were available.

Abby hitched her chair closer, her expression softening. "So you're not avoiding us? I mean, I know you've *seen* all of us over the last few months. . . ." She paused and exhaled slowly. "We just feel like we've done something wrong."

Tessa didn't know how she could explain. She didn't begrudge them their happy marriages. She just didn't feel like she belonged with them as much. Even when they didn't have their husbands around, the men were a major topic of conversation. Their children were discussed at least once an hour, even if they made a promise not to bring them up. And when they did shift away from their families, they often ended up teasing her about when she would find a man. Or if she had already found one . . .

She knew they didn't do it to hurt her. They probably didn't even realize that they were doing it. But their lives had changed.

And hers hadn't. Maybe that was the source of her frustration. She had been born and raised in Durant. Except for her years at college, she had never been away for an extended period of time. She still lived in the same house her parents had bought the year they were married.

Maybe she had made the wrong decision. The tourism business was flourishing in the Ozarks and she could have located her shop anywhere. But her roots were in Durant and she had come back, finding the empty building on Main Street the perfect site for the dream she had nurtured since high school.

"Hello, Tessa? Earth to Tessa."

She came back to the present to see Abby waving her hand in front of her face. She blinked and gave a self-conscious laugh. "Sorry."

"See, that's what we're talking about. Mandy or Christine might start to daydream in the middle of a conversation but you've always been the levelheaded one."

Maybe I'm tired of always being the levelheaded one, she wanted to snap, but she bit the words back before they slipped over her lips. She had been friends with Abby for too long to let a blue funk spoil it now.

"I'm really sorry," she said, scooting her chair around until she was facing Abby. "I honestly didn't mean to miss the evening. I just forgot."

Abby reached over and clasped Tessa's hands loosely between her own. "Tessa, are you sure things are okay?"

"Positive." She carefully disentangled her hands. "Listen, go back and tell everyone that I'm hosting a special get-together at my house this Thursday."

Abby laughed and hopped off the chair, her bubbly expression once more in place. "That would be great! I'll let Christine and Mandy know. We'll be there at seven with the food and the movie."

"Something good and weepy," Tessa said. Maybe a good cleansing cry would take care of this strange mood she was in.

She spent the next two evenings straightening the house and working in the back bedroom on a surprise for her three friends. She didn't want to think of it as an apology but she had been locking her friends out recently. Maybe if she talked to them, told them about her strange mood swings, they could help her figure out what was going on.

The activity kept her occupied and she didn't find her mind wandering as much while she sewed. When Fern suggested she go home early on Thursday, she decided to reward herself with an afternoon off.

"It shouldn't be too busy," she said as she gathered her purse and umbrella. "If you need anything, call. I'll be home."

"But it's such a lovely day," Fern said. "You should be outside, work in your garden, take a bike ride."

Being outside sounded inviting. With her parents coming home again soon, the garden could use some work. "I might do that. I'll see you tomorrow."

Once home, she changed into a pair of cut-off shorts and a workshirt of her father's. Rolling up the sleeves, she carried her gardening basket and the phone outside. Humming, she knelt down and started weeding the flower beds her mother had planted that spring.

The phone rang at 3:00. She finished digging out a stubborn weed nestled next to the roses and tossed it onto her pile before picking up the phone. Expecting Fern with a question, she was surprised to hear Mandy's croaking voice.

"What's the matter?" she asked, dropping her towel and squatting on her haunches.

"I'm not sure but I might have strep," Mandy managed, her voice hoarse and rough. "Greg wants me to come down for a throat culture. Granny Becca already picked up the kids. I'm sorry, Tessa, but I can't make it tonight."

"That's fine, honey. You just take care of yourself."

Hanging up the phone, she moved around the side of the house. A few clouds had darkened the sky, bringing with them the threat of rain, but she had only the bed of petunias left to weed. She could finish, take a quick shower, and be ready before Christine and Abby arrived.

A robin flew down from the oak tree and pecked at the

ground she had stirred up. Tugging a worm out of the soft soil, it flew away in triumph. Tessa leaned back, shading her eyes against the clouded sun, watching the bird settle in the tree. The phone rang again and she reached behind, clicking the ON button as she raised it to her ear.

"Hello."

"Hi, Tessa."

"Abby. Don't tell me you're canceling, too?" Her lips curved as she teased her friend and she rotated her sore shoulder muscles. A hot shower would feel great.

"What do you mean?"

"Mandy thinks she has strep. She sounded horrible. Greg's going to do a throat culture and the kids are staying with Rebecca."

"I almost envy her."

Tessa frowned at Abby's frustrated tone. "You want to be sick?"

"At least then my mother-in-law might not stop by."

Tessa grinned, understanding her friend's mood. Abby loved her in-laws but even without a toddler and a new baby, her housekeeping skills couldn't compete with her mother-in-law. Fortunately, Tim's parents had retired to Florida and Abby didn't have to deal with the situation on a daily basis. But no matter how many times her friends told her not to worry, she went on a cleaning binge just before their visit.

"When are they getting here?"

"Tomorrow evening. I thought I had a few more days but they made better time than they expected."

Tessa sighed. "So you're cleaning tonight?"

"I'm sorry, Tessa." Her remorse was evident. "You know I'd rather come to your house than clean. And after that scene in your office . . ."

"It's okay, Abby. You know, you don't have to worry about their visit. They just want to see you and their grand-kids."

"I know, I know. But I just can't get over it. I don't want her to think I'm a slob."

Tessa laughed. "You are not a slob, Abby. A little clutter never hurt anyone."

Abby promised she wouldn't back out next time and hung up. Tessa finished the last flowerbed, dusted off her knees, and carried her supplies onto the back porch.

She was washing her hands in the large sink when the phone rang again. By now, Fern would have closed the shop and gone home. Resigned to hearing Christine's voice, she didn't even blink when she heard the hesitant hello.

"Anna or Jake?" she asked before Christine could say anything else.

"What?"

"Are you canceling because of your daughter or your husband? That's the only excuse I haven't heard yet."

"What are you talking about?"

Tessa cradled the phone between her shoulder and ear and dried her hands. "Mandy can't come tonight because she's sick. Abby's frantically cleaning the house for a visit from her in-laws. I assume either Jake or Anna are sick. You are calling to cancel, aren't you?"

"Oh, Tessa, Abby and Mandy called already? Oh, I feel terrible."

"Don't. It's not like I went to any special trouble," she lied. "The house needed a good cleaning anyway."

"No, it isn't Jake or Anna. One of the nurses called in sick. Emily's going to cover for part of the night but she leaves on vacation tomorrow and she needs to pack. Jake isn't home yet but I could come over with Anna for a little while."

Tessa hesitated. She wouldn't be alone with Christine and Anna. But having the little girl over wouldn't be the same as enjoying an evening with her friends. And she wouldn't be able to talk about her conflicting emotions around the curious little girl.

"You know what? Maybe we should just cancel tonight," she said. "It's not our regular night anyway."

"Are you sure? I could pick up a pizza and get a movie."

Tessa knew she wasn't in the mood for one of the movies that Anna could watch. "No, I think I'll pass this week. If it's okay with you."

She hung up the phone and wandered into the living room. Four fat pillows leaned against the couch. Nudging the one decorated with stethoscopes and other medical symbols, she sighed.

She had been looking for curtain material when she found the medical pattern and immediately thought of Christine. The numbers for Abby had been easy to find and she had no trouble locating an alphabet pattern for Mandy. Her own design had eluded her for awhile until she found a bolt of material with outlines of antique furniture. The pillows had been fun to stitch up and she had looked forward to seeing her friends' faces when they walked into the room.

She carried the pillows into the small bedroom she had converted into her study/sewing room and stacked them against the wall. "Next time," she said out loud.

Nothing caught her fancy in the kitchen and she remembered Christine's offer to bring over a pizza. She dialed the number of the only pizza parlor in town and listened to the busy signal before hanging up.

The third time she heard the buzz, she grabbed her jacket and purse. She would have better luck ordering in person.

Only a few tables held patrons. One employee sat behind the counter reading a book while the other one wiped down tables. "I thought you'd be packed or so busy you couldn't squeeze out another pizza," she said.

The young man closed his book and adjusted his hat. "No, not really."

"Your line's been busy the last fifteen minutes."

He turned around and groaned. He shifted the phone back into the cradle. "Matt! You didn't hang up the phone all the way!"

The boy wiping tables glanced over his shoulder. Tessa recognized the teenager who had led her to Luke's office. "Oops." He gave her a broad grin and she couldn't help smiling back at him.

The other boy sighed. "Sorry about that."

"It's okay," Tessa said. "I needed to get out of the house anyway."

He took her order and filled her soda glass. Carrying it with her, she found a booth in a corner where she could see the rest of the room and propped her feet on the empty bench across from her.

Her feet moved in time to the music playing on the juke-box and she leaned back, enjoying the relaxed atmosphere. The hum of conversation came from the tables across the way and she could hear the two boys arguing about their favorite baseball teams. Her eyelids lowered.

"Hey, sleepyhead!"

Jerked back to consciousness by the voice and the tug on her tennis shoes, she shifted on the bench and let her feet fall before raising her eyes. Luke leaned against the booth divider, his arms crossed over his chest and a broad smile on his face.

She wished she had thought to change her clothes before coming downtown. He wore khaki shorts and a blue knit shirt that emphasized the breadth of his shoulders. She self-consciously tugged her cut-offs lower.

She scooted around on the bench until she was sitting up straight and gave him a small grin. "Hi, Luke." Her heart thudded under her shirt, from being snapped awake, she told herself.

"I guess this is the place to be if you're looking for action," he said.

Glancing around the room, she saw that most of the tables had emptied while she was dozing. "It was busier," she assured him.

"I'll take your word for it." He slid into the empty seat across from her without waiting for an invitation. "What can a person do after eight P.M. in Durant?"

"You could go bowling."

He shook his head. "Not unless you're on a league. Open bowling ends at five."

She narrowed her eyes and thought. "The library?"

"Closes at six tonight."

She leaned her elbows on the table and rested her chin on her cupped hands, concentrating on the possibilities. "The stores usually close by five-thirty," she mused. "The gas station's open until ten," she offered.

He chuckled. "That's an idea. I could go buy a candy bar."

"Wait, there has to be something else." She answered his smile with one of her own. "Pizza?"

He snapped his fingers. "Bingo! Which is why we're both here, right?"

"Actually, it's your sister's fault."

"Christine?"

Tessa nodded. "After she mentioned pizza, nothing in my cupboards sounded appetizing."

She moved her arms off the table when Matt delivered her pizza. She stared at the huge pan and then at Matt. "I ordered this?"

"You said large, didn't you?"

"I don't think . . ." Her voice trailed off. She was certain she had said medium but she couldn't embarrass the boy in front of Luke. "I must have been really hungry when I came in," she said, earning herself another grin from Matt. He must be devastating to the girls, she thought.

She nodded toward the pizza. "You haven't ordered yet, have you, Luke?"

"No."

"Then don't. There's no way I could eat all of this in a week."

Luke gave his drink order to Matt. "So, why aren't you eating pizza with Christine?"

Tessa picked up a piece of pizza and tugged the loose cheese away from the remaining pieces. "She has to take an extra shift tonight. What about you?"

"Didn't feel like sitting home."

"I bet it feels funny having your evenings free now that school's out."

He chewed off a bite and nodded. "Not that I don't enjoy my vacation but it takes a while to find a new rhythm."

A new rhythm. That was her problem, she thought. Her rhythm had always been connected to her friends. Now that they were married and had families, she hadn't found her own rhythm yet.

"Hey, thanks for helping with the house," he said. "Mom and Dad think it looks great."

"I know. Catherine called me the day after they came home." She nodded when Matt asked if she would like more soda. "Your idea turned out all right after all."

She chewed on her pizza, surprised at how comfortable she felt with Luke. Since the housewarming party, they hadn't been alone together. She didn't think she had done anything deliberately but somehow, they always managed to surround themselves with people.

"Things seem to be going pretty well with the Festival," he said.

She nodded, swallowing her bite. "Bessie said she has at least a dozen people interested in running food booths. She's going to bring a list to the meeting next week."

"Arthur said he would donate some items for prizes."

Tessa pressed her hand against her chest. "Be still my beating heart! Do you mean he's giving in?"

Luke grinned. "I think it's more a matter of, 'if you can't beat 'em, join 'em.' Or he's afraid he'll lose out completely if he doesn't do something."

A spot of tomato sauce clung to his chin and without thinking, she reached over and wiped it off with a napkin. Her thumb brushed against his skin and electricity arced between them.

Time stopped. She couldn't move, her hand halfway between his face and the table, mesmerized by the suddenly intense look in his eyes.

"So, you guys done?"

Matt's voice broke the spell and she dropped her hand to her lap.

"I'm full," she said, her eyes on the napkin she was crumbling into little pieces. "Luke?"

"Tessa," he said, his voice so concerned she lifted her head. His eyes crinkled at the corners, his twinkle once more apparent. "Please tell me you ate your share of the pizza. I don't think I could stand it if I ate more than half."

Tessa stared at the empty pan Matt was carrying away. Not even a crumb left. "I can't believe that. I never eat that much."

"You just needed the right company." He dug out his wallet and tossed several bills on the table. He handed her one but she lifted her hand and waved it away.

"You don't owe me anything."

"But we ate all your pizza. You could have eaten some of it for lunch tomorrow. I didn't mean to mooch."

She slid out of the booth. "You didn't. You saved me from looking like a pig."

Calling good-bye to the boys, Luke held the door open. She edged around him. Her shoulder brushed against his arm and her heart skittered. Unable to look at him, her knees wobbly, she breathed a sigh of relief when she was outside and could put several feet between them.

"Thanks for sharing dinner with me," she said.

"Would you like to take a walk?" he asked. "Walk off some of those calories."

She hesitated, her throat dry. If she told him no, he would know she was bothered by what had just happened.

Not that anything had happened. A tiny shock when their skin touched. After all, this was Luke. Her best friend's brother.

So what? that tiny imp in her brain said. *That argument is wearing a little thin. He's a man, isn't he? And just touching him for the barest moment sets off more fireworks than any of the kisses you've had with Gary.*

Aware that he was still waiting for her answer, she nodded. "That would be fine." Her hands in her pockets and her shoulders hunched up to her ears, she followed him across the street and toward the main part of town.

The stores were closed. They wandered down the deserted street, their voices hushed as they commented on the various sales posted in the windows. The easy camaraderie of earlier was gone and Tessa wondered how soon she could politely excuse herself and go back home.

Luke paused in front of Treasure Seekers' Haven. "I like your display. It looks inviting."

"Thanks." Tessa peered at the furniture cozily arranged inside the window. "Fern did this one."

"I'm impressed."

"I'll tell her."

He caught her arm. "No, I'm impressed you let her do the display. You've always been a little possessive about your shop."

She gently disengaged herself from his touch. A ripple had started under his fingers and she was finding it difficult to breathe. "I just had to find the right person. Fern loves the place as much as I do."

Turning away, she saw a light from the back room. "Oh, the office light's still on." She dug in her purse and pulled out her keychain.

"You don't have to wait," she said to Luke, hoping he would leave so she could return to her normal self. She didn't like these feelings he was stirring in her.

"I don't mind. I'll come in with you just in case."

"Just in case?" She unlocked the deadbolt and the lock and pushed the door open, waiting until he was inside before locking it again.

"In case it's not just a matter of the light being left on."

"A burglar?" She led the way between the furniture, as

familiar with the layout here as at her house. "I've never had a robbery."

"That doesn't mean you won't. They happen in small towns, too, you know."

"You sound just like my mother," she said, grinning at him over her shoulder as she turned toward the office.

Her foot tripped over a low table that hadn't been there that morning. Her cry of surprise was stifled as she felt Luke's arms wrap around her waist.

He eased her onto a low stool. "Are you okay?"

"I think so." She rubbed her hand over her foot and grimaced when she touched her ankle.

"What is it?"

"My ankle."

He knelt down in front of her. The office light trickled through the beaded curtain, barely illuminating them. The back of his hair swept the top of his shirt collar and she caught a whiff of his aftershave when he shifted closer to her.

She tried to move away but he had her shoe in his hands. He carefully moved her foot back and forth. "Does that hurt?"

"No." Pain was not the sensation she was experiencing.

He probed the area above her sock with gentle fingers. His touch drifted over her ankle bone and she jolted. "Ow!"

"I think it's just bruised." He carefully rolled down her sock and lightly tapped the sensitive skin above the bone with his fingertips. She gritted her teeth and clutched the edges of the footstool.

"You'd be rolling and groaning if it was sprained or broken," he said, smoothing her sock back into place.

She was surprised she wasn't rolling and groaning. What

was he doing to her? "I'll have you know, I'm pretty tough."

His face was only inches away from her and her pulse jumped. A shiver of excitement raced down her spine.

His eyelids lowered and her breath caught in her throat at his expression. She swallowed twice. "Fern must have moved this stool today," she said breathlessly.

I can't do this, I can't do this. I don't have time for a relationship, he's Christine's brother, what if things don't work out?

His knuckles lightly brushed over her cheek, wiping away all her reasons to not get involved. "Your eyes are so lovely," he said quietly. "So dark. Like the night sky before the stars come out."

Her fingers tingled against the embroidered pattern of the footstool she still clutched. "How . . . how poetic."

One finger followed the path of her jawline. "Your skin is so soft." His finger trailed over her lips. "And your lips . . ."

The kiss was whisper-soft, a mere brushing of lips against lips. But she felt the power of it surging through her, melding her with him, bringing them close even though their bodies never touched.

Her eyes fluttered closed and she sighed. The muffled sound echoed through the room. His lips touched hers again and she swayed toward him. He tasted of the outdoors, of the pepperoni pizza they had shared, of soft summer nights.

The kiss lasted forever and only a minute. He backed away and she slowly opened her eyes, blinking before she could focus. His finger tapped against her lips. "We need to check on the light," he said softly.

"What?"

"Your office light." He stood up and pulled her to her

feet, keeping one hand linked with hers as he led her toward the back of the shop.

She clicked off the lamp and let him lead her back to the front door. Dazed, she was grateful for his guidance, the firm grip of his hand on hers.

What was the matter with her? She'd been kissed before. Maybe not with that same gentle touch, almost as if she were cherished. She glanced at Luke's profile, barely visible in the shadowed room. Why had she never seen this gentle side of him before?

I wasn't looking, she told herself. *I only saw him as Christine's older brother.*

He stopped at the front door and waited while she twisted the locks open. On the other side, he tucked his hands in his jacket pockets while she locked up again.

"I probably should get home," she said, uncertain what to say now that they were standing in the full glare of the street light. He stood a foot away from her, his hands securely in his pockets, and all her rational reasons for staying away from him came back.

"Yeah, me, too."

They walked back to the pizza parlor without speaking. A car passed them, its engine overly loud in the quiet night. Their footsteps echoed through the street as they each walked back quietly, lost in their own thoughts.

Why did he kiss me? she thought, her system still alive with the sensations his touch had awakened. She slanted a glance at him but he was staring in front of him, his pace purposeful as he marched toward the pizza parlor. His fingers drummed a steady pattern against his pant leg.

She could see nothing of the man who had so tenderly kissed her back at the shop. *He's trying to figure out how to tell me it was a mistake,* she thought, a pang starting in her heart and spreading throughout her body. A momentary lapse in a secluded setting.

They reached her car. Luke turned toward her. "About what happened—"

"Don't worry about it," she interrupted quickly, determined to dismiss it first.

He frowned. "What?"

Her pulse fluttered in her throat like a trapped bird. *Make it short and sweet and get out of here. You don't want to cry in front of him.* "I like you a lot, Luke. You've always been like a big brother to me. That doesn't have to change."

"I see." He rubbed a hand over his jaw. "Well, then, good night."

He spun on his heel and climbed in his car, driving away before she even managed to open her door. As his lights disappeared in the distance, she wondered when the temperature had dropped.

Chapter Ten

Tessa studied the figures in front of her, their shapes blurring on the paper. Rubbing a hand over her eyes, she leaned back in her chair and stared at the ceiling. "I need a walk," she muttered to Fern.

"Go ahead, dear." Fern smiled when Tessa stood up. "We've been quiet today so I shouldn't have any problem handling whatever comes up."

"You could handle anything." Tessa paused in the doorway. "In fact, as soon as this festival is over, what do you think about handling it all by yourself?"

Fern's smile disappeared. "By myself?" She pressed a hand to her chest.

Tessa nodded. "You're more than ready. And everybody's been after me to go on a vacation. I might just go out to Seattle and rummage through Aunt Sylvia's attic myself." But I'll definitely stay away from any wedding dresses, she vowed silently.

Her mind wandered as she walked down the sidewalk toward the far end of the downtown area. Over the last two days, she had found it difficult to keep anything on her mind for more than a few moments. Bessie and Mabel had come into the store yesterday and given her some details about the festival and she had embarrassed herself by asking them to repeat everything at least twice.

Deep down, she knew why. The thought twisted and turned inside her but she couldn't take it out, not yet. Crossing the street, she stuffed her hands in the front pockets of her cotton slacks and frowned at the ground. How could she be such a coward with Luke? His kiss had been a surprise, but to totally ignore it like that . . . it would serve her right if he never talked to her again.

She bumped into a solid figure and lifted her head. Gary smiled, his hands gently holding onto her elbows. "Heavy thoughts?"

Now why couldn't he be the one who made her insides tingle? she thought irritably. Life would be less complicated, without all these maddening ups and down.

Some of her feelings must have shown on her face because his smile faltered. "Are you okay?"

She forced her lips to curve upward. "Just taking a breather." She carefully withdrew from his hold. "So, how have you been?"

"Fine." His glance swept across her face. "Tessa, what's going on?"

She tossed her braid over her shoulder. "Nothing, why?"

He studied her for a few more seconds and then grabbed her hand. "Come on, this has gone on long enough."

Before she realized what he was doing, he had led her into his law practice, past the empty secretary's desk, and into the small room that served as his private office, seating her on a comfortable chair opposite his desk. He sat down in the matching chair across from her.

"Tessa, I've watched you the last few days. You're not yourself. You have to make a decision."

He couldn't know, could he? "About what?"

He rested his elbows on the arms of his chair and steepled his fingers together, tapping his index fingers against his chin until she thought she would scream. "Luke or me," he finally said.

A soft gasp escaped her. "What?"

"You know what I'm talking about."

She held herself still, determined not to squirm under his scrutiny. "I don't think I want to have this conversation," she managed to say. "We've gone out a few times, Gary, but I'm not ready for anything else." She took a deep breath and released it slowly. "I didn't think you were, either."

"I didn't think I was." He hesitated and then leaned forward, his mouth only inches away from hers. "Since I've been seeing you, though—"

"It's Durant," she broke in quickly, edging backwards until she bumped up against the soft cushion of the chair. "With everyone getting married, having babies, you feel like you're the only one left out. . . ."

Her voice trailed off as his hand gently cupped the side of her face. "Be quiet," he said softly.

His kiss was gentle, tender.

And nothing else.

His finger under her chin, he gently tipped her head up until their eyes met. "What just happened?"

She blinked. "You kissed me."

"And?"

"And?" she repeated, her eyes wide, knowing what he wanted but unable to give it to him. Even though she now knew without question she loved Luke, she couldn't hurt Gary's feelings.

"Any bells or whistles?"

She stared at him a moment. His gaze was intent and she knew she couldn't lie to him. "No," she whispered.

He sighed and dropped his hand to his lap, leaning back in his chair. "Are you using me to make Luke Hunter jealous?"

"No!" His question shocked the word out of her. "I would never . . . how could you think such a thing . . ."

He lifted his hand and gave her a weary smile. "I didn't think you were. After Hunter's running tip, I wondered, but over the last few weeks . . ."

Her eyes narrowed suspiciously. "What running tip?"

He grinned, his face relaxing for the first time since they had entered his office. "It was actually very clever. Highway 14 abounds with dogs. Dogs who aren't chained up and don't like runners."

She frowned. "Luke told you to run on that road so you would get hurt?"

Gary shook his head. "Not get hurt. Just have a little extra workout. I think he was marking his turf." His grin widened. "An appropriate metaphor, I would say."

"That's awful." She crossed her arms over her chest. "And just like him."

She might love him but she had no illusions. The woman Luke Hunter loved would have to develop a strong sense of the ridiculous. And while she didn't know yet how she was going to accomplish it, she was going to be that woman.

"I don't blame him," Gary said softly, his expression serious again.

This time, she did squirm under his look. "Gary."

"I think you should tell him."

"Tell him what?"

"Tessa." His tone implied that she wasn't fooling him. She sighed. "I can't."

"Why not?" He swiveled around in his chair and propped his feet on his desk. "If you love him, why not just tell him? Why all this dodging around?"

"Because . . ." She hesitated, not sure what to say, not sure why she was even talking about this with him. "Because what if he doesn't love me!" she finally blurted. "I could ruin my friendship with Christine."

Gary stared at her and then started laughing. She frowned. "What's so funny?"

"If I didn't know better, I'd think you were blind."

She fisted her hands on her hips. "What's that supposed to mean?"

He shook his head, gaining control of his laughter. "Tessa, just look at the way he watches you. He cares about you. If he has the intelligence I think he does, he loves you."

A warm glow spread through Tessa. "Really?"

"Really." He shook his head. "I can't even believe I'm having this conversation with you."

"Maybe you're more a counselor than you realized," she offered.

He shook his head. "No, I think I'm just a fool." He stood up and pulled her to her feet, planting a soft, brotherly kiss on her forehead. The kind she realized now she had never received from Luke. "Since it's Saturday, I assume Hunter is at his house. Why don't you go over there and put him out of his misery?"

Her heart fluttered. "Are you sure?"

"I'm sure. A wise man knows when it's time to fold his

hand and walk away." He gave her a push toward the door. "And it's time you two acted like adults and sorted this out."

"It's time you two acted like adults and sorted this out."

Gary's words echoed in her mind as she drove the short distance to Luke's place. A gravel driveway at the side of his parents' house led toward the backyard and the entrance to his small apartment and she followed it carefully, pulling over before she reached the spot where he could see her from his window.

She parked the car and leaned her head on the steering wheel. How had this happened? Falling in love wasn't part of her plan. She had things to do, places to see . . .

And to fall in love with Luke, of all people!

"Right," she muttered, letting loose a long sigh. "Tessa Montgomery, be honest with yourself for once. You've never stopped loving the guy."

And what was she going to say now? "Oh, by the way, Luke, I think the reason I've been so annoying to you all these years, especially these last few months, is because I love you. I used my relationship with Christine as my excuse to not show you but I think it's time to get this in the open. You wouldn't by any chance feel the same way?"

She groaned and thumped her head on the steering wheel.

A light tapping on the window startled her and she jerked her head up. Luke stood outside the window, dressed in running clothes. His skin glistened from his exercise.

She reached over and rolled down the window. "Hi," she managed weakly.

Her heart pounded under her shirt. She wouldn't be surprised if he could hear it.

"Hi." He gave her a puzzled smile. "What are you doing here?"

"I, um . . ." She paused and opened her mouth to give him the information Bessie and Mabel had shared yesterday and then Gary's words reverberated around her brain again. "I think we need to talk," she said.

"Okay."

She could hear the reluctance in his voice. *He doesn't want to talk to me,* she thought sadly. All these years of pushing him away had finally done the trick.

She opened the door and stepped out, noticing that he quickly backed away from her until several feet separated them. Her heart broke just a little more.

But she wouldn't be able to live with herself if she didn't make an attempt.

"I'm pretty sweaty," he said. "You don't want to get too close."

He led her around the side of the house to the patio that provided him with some outdoor privacy. "Mom and Dad went to Kansas City for the weekend," he said as he unfolded two lawn chairs for them. "They took Anna to the zoo."

Tessa nodded in relief, taking the chair he handed her. At least her humiliation wouldn't be witnessed by anyone else.

But Gary was right. It was time to get this out in the open.

Suddenly she knew what she needed to do. She clutched the back of her chair. "Close your eyes."

"Tessa, if this is your idea of a joke—"

"No," she interrupted, fearing her resolve would disappear quickly. "This won't take long. Please."

He searched her face closely and she stood still, wondering if he could see what she had been hiding even from herself for so long. *I love you,* she said silently, praying for the courage to say it out loud, no matter the consequences.

"This better be good," he muttered and closed his eyes.

Taking a deep breath and releasing it quickly, she moved around until she was directly in front of him, stood on her tiptoes, and pressed her lips against his, tasting the salt of his perspiration, absorbing his heat.

Luke jerked away from her, his eyes flashing open. One of the lawn chairs clattered to the ground. "What is this?"

"Tell me what happened, Luke."

"What happened?" He stared at her as if she had lost her mind. "You kissed me."

She nodded, her heart pounding so hard she was afraid it would jump right out of her body. Surely if he didn't care, he would be calmer. "Were there any bells or whistles?"

His eyes narrowed. "What are you doing?"

She clenched her hands together and pressed them against her stomach. "It's an experiment. When I kissed Gary earlier . . ." His face hardened and a tiny spurt of hope leapt to life. ". . . there weren't any bells or whistles. Not even a tiny toot. But with you, just now, I could hear the whole seventy-six trombones."

An eyebrow arched upward. "Seventy-six trombones, huh?" One corner of his mouth twitched.

She nodded. "I've been fighting you, Luke, and myself. Over the last few weeks, I think . . . well," she swallowed and her voice tightened up again. "I, ah . . ." She couldn't say it. Not knowing would at least let her pretend they could have a happy ending. At least for a little while.

But she wasn't a coward. And if he didn't love her now,

she could wait, give him time. "I've discovered I love you," she finished in a rush.

A broad grin broke out on his face and he wrapped his arms around her middle, spinning her around the small patio, her feet knocking the chairs to the cement with a clatter. "Finally! Do you know how long I've waited to hear those words from you?"

She stared at him, still not sure she understood him right. "Does that mean . . . ?"

His kiss swallowed the rest of her question. When he finally lifted his head, she had to hold on to him to keep from dropping to the ground in a puddle.

"Why didn't you say anything?" she asked when she could finally breathe again.

"And have you laugh in my face?" He brushed tiny kisses all over her face. "I tried, Tessa. But after all those years of treating you like a pesky kid, I didn't think you'd believe I'd had a complete turnaround. A wise man knows when it's better to be quiet."

"I've had about enough of this wise man talk," she grumbled. "A wise man knows when to put up his cards. A wise man knows when it's better to be quiet. Who is this wise man, anyway?"

"I'd like to think it was me." His arms tightened around her and she saw her own love reflected in his eyes. Why had she fought her feelings so long?

"Come on," he said. "I want to try an experiment of my own."

Even if she loved him, he was still Luke. "What?" she asked carefully.

"I want to see if we can bring on the entire brass band."

Epilogue

"What do you think?" Luke shouted over the hand clapping and foot stomping of the audience waiting for Natalie Upman to come on stage.

Tessa cupped her hand around her mouth. "I'm going to be deaf in the morning."

He laughed and wrapped an arm around her waist, hugging her close. "You're loving every minute of this."

She grinned and leaned into him, relishing the moment and inhaling his scent through the aromas of the food vendors.

A hot August sun beat down on the crowd gathered in the middle of the street. A drummer and guitarist sat on the makeshift stage, their warm-up music barely noticeable over the noise of the crowd.

A deafening roar went up and Tessa pushed her hand on Luke's shoulder to raise herself higher. The rays of the sun sparkled on the diamond ring she wore. "There she is!" she called excitedly.

Mabel walked beside the pretty young woman, the older woman's face wreathed in smiles. She raised her hands and patted the air several times until the noise subsided. "Ladies and gentlemen, welcome to the first annual Durant Founders Day Festival. It's now my privilege to introduce my cousin . . . Natalie Upman!"

The crowd cheered and then the band struck the first chords. Natalie belted out the words of a love she never thought to find, a love to last all time. . . .

"Wow!"

Tessa grinned at Luke's thunderstruck expression. "She's got quite the voice for such a little thing, doesn't she?" she asked.

He nodded and then nudged her arm, pointing toward the far end of the street. "Look over there."

She turned her head. Arthur Owens stood in front of his shop, his mouth open. When he saw her staring at him, he lifted both hands in a gesture of capitulation and gave her a thumbs-up.

She waved, her happiness spilling over. "I never dreamed it would be this good."

His arm tightened around her waist. "I did."

Her heart slowed and then raced faster. He wasn't talking about the festival. "All those years," she murmured, dropping her head on his shoulder, still amazed at the love that flowed between them.

"So, you sure you don't want to move up the wedding?" he whispered.

Her heart skipped a beat. "Mom only has six weeks as it is. And Aunt Sylvia's dress is still at the cleaners."

He leaned back, his eyes roving over the sundress and sandals she wore. "This dress looks fine. We could get married tonight."

She blushed and ducked her head at the longing she saw in his eyes. "You nut."

He squeezed her waist. "If we wait until September, we can't have a honeymoon until Thanksgiving."

"Then we can finish redecorating the house." A week after the wedding, they would sign the final loan papers to buy her childhood home from her parents. "Besides, aren't you the one who said that you didn't need to go anywhere for a vacation?" She tipped her head to one side, frowning in concentration. "I'm sure you said something like that when Seth came back."

He groaned. "Why do you have such a good memory?"

Images of their times together drowned out the music around her. Now that she knew he loved her, so much made sense. Being on the committee so that they could be together. Not touching her so that she wouldn't guess how he really felt about her. Hiding his feelings behind nicknames and teasing comments.

"Fern was right," she said in astonishment.

"What?"

She raised her head until her lips were next to his ear. "I can't believe I never knew how you felt about me. Even Fern knew."

He twisted his head and gave her a quick, hard kiss. "You weren't ready. If I'd pressed you earlier, you would have run away."

She considered his words and then nodded. "How'd you get so smart?"

" 'Cause I spend so much time in school!" He grabbed

her hands and swung her around in time to the fast-paced song Natalie was now singing. "Come on, Tessa, this is dancing music!"

Her heart full, she matched his rhythm, step by step.